The Miracle Inspector

Helen Smith

TYGER BOOKS

A CIP catalogue record for this book is available
from the British Library.

ISBN 978-0956517050

Tyger Books
an imprint of Emperors Clothes Ltd
28 Rosebery Road
London SW2 4DD
United Kingdom

Cover illustration by Ian Dodds

This book is for Lauren

1 Breakfast

Lucas was dressed smartly, ready for work. He sat at the kitchen table and buttered his toast, and cracked at the top of the boiled egg his wife had made him for breakfast. Angela stood nearby, scrubbing at a small spot on the working surface. Layers of regret hung between them like unfashionable wallpaper. It made the place seem ugly.

'You know what would be nice?' Angela said.

Lucas didn't answer. He was not being impolite, he was waiting for her to express her feelings.

She said, 'If we could go somewhere…'

He didn't speak. He licked his fingers. He couldn't eat the egg but he ate his toast. He waited for her to continue.

'…together. I wish there was something…'

He noticed that she had stopped rubbing the spot, as if speaking the words had been helping to power her hand. Or perhaps it was the other way around. He'd have liked to make a joke of it. Would the nub of it – the joke – be something about kinetic energy?

'Will you be home for your tea?' she said.

'Yes,' he said. He wiped his hands and brushed himself down, preparing to leave her. With his weary, cautious manner, his formal clothes, he could have been forty-five years old. He was not quite twenty-five.

'Unless there's a miracle?'

'Well, then you definitely wouldn't have to cook tea.' He laughed, thinking they would share a moment.

She stared blankly back at him.

'If I discovered a miracle, you'd come and see it,' he said. 'Wouldn't you?'

She set to work on that spot on the working surface again. She loved her husband; it had been a love match, not forced. There'd probably be only four or five years before one or other of them fell foul of the authorities, so she ought to treasure their time together. But most of their time 'together' was spent alone, and the dull routine of running a household was wearing her down. She was making a study of dinosaurs from the encyclopaedias she had salvaged when the local library closed down. Memorising the long names kept her mind occupied, with decisions about how to pronounce the multiple syllables providing a counterpoint to mundane tasks like shaking out the mat, folding linen, polishing taps. Recent attempts to use the recitation of dinosaur names and characteristics as a method of timing the preparation of the egg she boiled each morning for Lucas's breakfast had thus far ended in failure.

Angela rubbed and rubbed at the spot on the working surface even though she could no longer see it. This was her life for the foreseeable future. She was not quite twenty-one years old.

That evening, when Lucas came home again, Angela didn't even ask him how his day went. What made her so sure he hadn't found anything, that it wasn't worth asking about his day? What if he had the secret with him now, the beautiful, pure, shining truth of it? How would he put it? He was no good with words. 'Darling, I've got some wonderful news. You must keep it to yourself for now.' Would she think it was a good thing? He realised with a blush that she might not like him to use the word 'darling'. It was silly and old-fashioned. He didn't like it much himself – it reminded him of that old reprobate, Jesmond.

'It's a bit dry,' Angela said to him. She was talking about the fish she had put on the plates for their evening meal. She could have been talking about their relationship. How could he put that in a lighthearted way, without seeming critical or prurient, inviting comparisons with wetness, which she wouldn't approve of, and which he hadn't actually meant to suggest? After some consideration, he said nothing.

'You could have called me today.'

'I couldn't, not really.'

'They didn't have phones wherever you were?'

If I knew a secret, I would keep it for you. That's what he wanted to say. It seemed too craven. He tried to bring some sunshine in to the room. He thought about what it would be like to sit on some grass somewhere, looking at the light on her face. 'Maybe we could have a holiday. Would you like that? Richmond or Highgate or somewhere nice. You choose.'

He watched her thinking about what he said, chewing it over in her mind, trying to break it down and make it digestible. She even moved her jaw a little, as if she had a mouth full of hi-fibre bread and was finding it difficult to despatch. But she didn't reply.

The silences were not something he had expected from marriage. Sex, yes. Companionship. Someone to cook a meal and sit down and eat with, that kind of thing. The silences had evolved naturally, a way of being: 'Our silences', yet with no emptiness or vacancy in them. Instead, there were whole worlds contained in those silences; millions of gossamer strands of understanding going back and forth between them, like an invisible version of that fibreglass loft insulation that was illegal now. At school, his art teacher had explained to him that if he wanted to draw something, a chair, for example, he shouldn't look only at what he could see – the structure of the thing – but also at the spaces. Sometimes it helped to draw the spaces. Similarly, in conversations with his wife, Lucas felt that to acknowledge only the words that were said would have been unhelpful. Their relationship was also about the silences.

He wanted a way to tell her out loud that he loved her and that her silences warmed him like invisible now-illegal loft insulation. But he couldn't. It would only have come out sounding like a chorus from one of those Country and Western parody acts that were briefly popular on the radio a few years ago, before radio stations were banned and all the apparatus in London confiscated.

That was what he was thinking. What was she thinking?

How long had they been married? It seemed to him that he had never before wondered what she was thinking – although that was impossible, and he must have wondered and then forgotten about it. When she spoke, he listened and then reacted to the words he heard her say. Too often he was briefly wounded by the awfulness of what she said. Later, he would find a way of being reassured by it; it was just 'her way'. Had he never before stopped to wonder if there was any subtext to what she said, to wonder whether she struggled with silly thoughts that she hid from him, the way he hid his thoughts from her? He didn't remember ever doing so. He was too preoccupied with keeping his thoughts hidden to worry about hers.

If he could prise open her head with a penknife and put a straw into her brain and siphon out the thoughts, suck them up and then drip them out on to a specially-prepared surface in front of him in a legible little puddle, so he could pick them over and examine them – well, he would have been surprised to uncover anything more profound than the expression of simple wants, needs and instructions to herself that would enable her to carry out her daily tasks around the house: 'Bread, table. Knives, forks, spoons, salt. Toilet. Eat. Drink. Sex.' That sort of thing. And yet she was an intelligent woman. It was extraordinary to him that he had never realised that she might have a secret life, something she kept away from him. Did she ever share these thoughts with anyone else? A friend? A 'relative'? A journal?

'What?'

'Sorry?'

'You're just sitting there, staring. Finish your meal. Don't you like it?'

'What were you thinking about?'

'You were the one sitting there not saying anything,' she said. 'I was only wondering what you were thinking about.'

'I was wondering what sort of thing you think about.' He felt slightly defeated by it all but to his surprise she laughed girlishly, as if he'd just made a rather wonderful joke. 'I have these thoughts sometimes,' he said. 'Things I want to say to you that sound like poetry in my head. And I stop myself because they wouldn't come out right.'

'Like what?' A little nostril flare of suspicion from her.

He pressed on: 'I was going to say to you that I don't mind it when we don't say much to each other. It's like being wrapped up in loft insulation. That's all.'

He expected her to laugh again. But she stared at him for a few seconds as if he had just said something rather vulgar. Then she came over to him and kissed him once, very gently, on the mouth. Then she half sat on his leg, turned and pushed away the plate of half-eaten food, turned back to him and kissed him, putting her tongue in his mouth – did he taste of the food? – while grinding herself against him. He reached up under her shirt and pushed her bra up and felt her bare skin and then fumbled about – or they fumbled together – and got her knickers out of the way and his trousers undone and they had sex. It wasn't ideal because of the still-warm food on the plate and not brushing his teeth and the sadness he had noticed in her. She was behaving as if they had just met in a nuclear shelter and the sirens were still going. He put his mouth on her skin, about an inch along from her nipple and bit her. He did it quite gently and she didn't complain, as if she resisted letting him know anything about how she felt, even when she felt pain. Even when he caused it.

When they finished, she seemed giggly again. Happy, sad, happy. It was as if she was insane. 'You're not pregnant?'

'You want a miracle here, at home?' Now she was angry. Sometimes he felt he didn't know her at all. What was there to be angry about? Did she want a child? Or was she simply making a joke? Perhaps she had been making a joke, pretending to be angry, and it had misfired. He felt tired. Desperately tired, as if it was the end of everything, as if he had just carried home something expensive and heavy to save a child's life – an iron lung or some other breathing apparatus – only to find that the child had already died.

'If I was certified as a miracle,' she said, 'you'd have to stay here and guard me. We could make love all day, then.'

Jesus. She seemed to want to have sex again. She took her top off. She took her skirt off. She took her knickers off. She looked sad again. Maybe it was because he was sitting there gawping, in an appalled kind of way.

She took off his shirt, tugged at his trousers, tried to pull him on top of her.

'Not on the floor, you'll get cold,' he said.

She had one hand at the back of his neck, pulling his face down on hers so she could kiss him. She had her nose pressed right into his face.

'You're not crying?'

She didn't answer. But her face was damp with tears.

He got her up off the floor and half carried her into the living room. It was unromantic. He was like a soldier escorting a wounded colleague. He got her on to the sofa. Perhaps they should talk about things. He'd probably said something wrong. Or not said the right thing. Was it the loft insulation or the miracles, or the food that had dried out in the oven? Perhaps she'd hoped he'd make it home earlier today?

'I'm sorry,' he said. It seemed as good a start as any. But she just wanted to have sex again. She was lying on her back and she had her neck resting at an angle on the arm of the sofa. He was worried about snapping it. If he was too energetic and he accidentally snapped her neck and she died instantly but he carried on having sex with her... Actually, it wouldn't matter what people thought or if he went to prison because nothing would matter any more because his wife would have died, and he honestly

8

wouldn't want to live any more if she was dead. He thought the world of her.

'Angela,' he said afterwards, 'let's go away to Cornwall together.' It was the sort of thing people in London said to each other all the time these days, without having any idea of how they would get there or whether living in Cornwall would really be any better than living in London. But if you wanted to excite and flatter a woman you were supposed to mention Cornwall, as if there could be nothing finer than taking her to a place where she'd be expected to earn her living by serving behind the counter in a supermarket or whatever they made them do there.

But women were funny like that. They were just like other people – they always wanted what they hadn't got.

'Lucas,' she said. 'If I could really believe that…'

'About Cornwall?'

'Some days I think I can't bear another minute of it.'

'You sound like one of those women, in those war-time films, you know – with their marvellous accents "I simply can't bear another minute of it".'

'I can't stand another fucking minute of it. Is that clear enough for you? Is that unstoic enough? Don't say it if you don't mean it. How would we get to Cornwall?'

Was this a rhetorical question?

'With your job, you must know. How could we get to Cornwall? If you really meant it, Lucas, I'd go with you tomorrow.'

That's the thing. He didn't really mean it. For some reason that was mysterious even to him, he had used what was effectively a seduction line after he'd already had sex with her twice and without any urgent wish to do it for a third time, since he had a headache and his cock was a bit sore. It was unstrategic of him. He hadn't thought it through.

'Or Wales. We could go to Wales.' She wasn't going to let it go.

'I didn't know you wanted to go to Wales.'

'Anywhere but here. Imagine if we lived somewhere by the sea, with nice friends, no restrictions on where we went or what we did. Kids playing happily. Not wondering what I'd do if I gave birth to a girl because bringing a girl into this world is a curse.'

'What would I do for work?'

'I don't know.'

'That's the sort of thing you've got to worry about. How would I support us? Would they let us in to Cornwall?'

'We'd find a way. As for being accepted – you've got money. If we didn't ask for anything, only contributed...'

'OK, look. Don't get upset. Angela? Angela?' She looked as if she would cry again. 'Don't get upset. I'll look into it. I don't know how these things work. We've got money but there are currency restrictions. What if it doesn't have any value there?'

'Find something that does.'

'I'll look into it.'

'You've got friends in the Ministry.'

'I have.'

'You've got influence.'

'Was that why you married me?'

'What?'

'Did you think I had something? Money, power? A way out? Because I don't.'

'I married you for your blue eyes.'

'You know,' he said, 'sometimes I wonder if you're happy.'

'Happy? No, I'm not happy. Jesus. Of course I'm not happy. But that's hardly your fault. It's just the way things are.'

'You married me for my blue eyes?'

'You're sweet. I like the sex, the sex is great. Yeah, you've got money and the car and the house and all that. It's not about that, though, is it.'

'We could have a baby.'

No answer.

'Are you bored?'

'I'm not bored. I'm a prisoner. I want to leave here.'

'With me?'

'With you.'

'I love you, Angela.'

'I know.'

You can't say to someone – to your own wife, after she has revealed that she is deeply unhappy – you can't say 'So, do you love me, then?' It might sound needy. He had said 'I love you' to her. She should have said it back to him. It was accepted, to bat it back; a reflex. The table tennis of love. She didn't actually have to mean it. It was comforting, that's all.

'What?' Sometimes she looked at him as if she could hear his thoughts. Why couldn't he hear hers?

'Nothing. I love you, Angela.'

'I know.'

He'd have to try harder if he wanted her to say she loved him and mean it. A good job at the Ministry, sex most nights when he came home, money in the bank, food on the table – it wasn't enough for her. She wanted to be happy.

'Lucas?'

'I was thinking about Cornwall. I was thinking about us driving to the beach – about you driving, if you wanted to – and lying there on the sand, looking up at the sky, without anyone asking us what we were doing.'

'You really think it's like that?'

'A little house with a garden and a dog.'

'You're allowed dogs there?'

'Why not? And a couple of kids. And friends. Having dinner with friends.'

'I know the names I'd call my kids.'

'Do you?'

'Don't sound so surprised.'

'We've never discussed it.'

'You think I only think about the things that you discuss with me?'

'I'm not... you make me sound like an ogre. I don't make the rules. I don't think it's fair.'

'Don't you? Why don't you try and change it, then?'

It had never occurred to him before now that he might be married to a woman who was a seditionist. He felt a sickening shock of fear. His mouth flooded with a bitter taste, his breathing quickened. He picked up a napkin and put it to his mouth and drooled saliva into it, discreetly, to get rid of the taste. He lived in a misogynistic, patriarchal society but still, a man wasn't supposed to sit and drool on the floor in his own home. His hands felt damp and cold, and his fingers unresponsive, too weak to close in on themselves and make a fist around the napkin. A terrible thought had suddenly come into his head: what if she was a spy? What if she had been asked to say this by the Ministry? Where had he met her, anyway? What did he know about her, really? Maybe it was a test. Perhaps if he tried to have sex with her again? It might take her mind off it. Besides, she was probably feeling pretty horny with all this talk of Cornwall. He put his hands on her.

'Lucas. Don't do that. Are you listening to me? Are you saying we can go to Cornwall?'

'Yes.'

She put her arms around him and kissed him, dryly and gratefully, the way he'd seen her kiss a bottle opener once, after she'd spent half the day looking for it.

And that was it. She wasn't a spy, she was an unhappy girl and it was in his power to make her happy. He'd made a promise to her, the woman he loved more than anything in the world. All he needed now was a miracle, ha ha.

'I meant to tell you,' Angela said. 'Jesmond was here.'

'You meant to tell me?'

'He turned up around lunchtime.'

'You didn't let him in?'

'He was hungry, I had to give him a meal. He had a notebook full of old poems and stuff. Said you might want to look through it.'

'I'm not interested.'

She attempted an impersonation of Jesmond's slightly florid style of speaking: '"My dear, let me list all the things I wish I could have left with you: a small, shiny shell picked up on a beach on an outing with a woman I was in love with, a poem written for Matthew and Anna when Lucas was born, a photo of my mother, a postcard from my brother sent shortly before he was taken. I've lost them all along the way – all except this. Keep it safe for me. They'll want it for the archive one day, when the situation improves."'

'Oh. The archive!'

'You know he adores you.'

'If "adores" means turning up unannounced twice a year, stinking and skint and trying to cadge food off you while I'm out at work.'

'Don't be an arse.'

But Lucas was uneasy; you never knew who was watching the house.

2 The Ministry

The next morning Lucas drove through near-empty streets in the sleek, air-conditioned car that had been allocated to him when he first took up his job at the Ministry. He did the same journey every morning, and he never gave a thought any more to the disused runways at Heathrow that were filled with rusting rows of confiscated vehicles, although a glimpse, through tinted windows, of some Ministry employee engaged in a menial task – sweeping leaves at the side of the road or counting daisies in the grass verges – occasionally prompted an appreciation of his privileged position. But that day he saw no one except a few women scurrying along the pavements in their billowing black garments, heads down. And he didn't really notice them.

He parked the car right outside the Ministry building where he worked. It was difficult to imagine that the flaking yellow or red lines still visible along the edge of some of the streets he drove through, or the zebra stripes that spanned them, had once had some purpose other than purely decorative; that, like the coloured lights on poles at the junctions and the risibly childish symbols on the metal signs at the side of the road, they had once been used to control the flow of traffic and to advise drivers about how and where to park. He could no more imagine streets full of traffic than he could imagine skies full of planes.

He walked up the steps at the entrance to the Ministry building and into the marble lobby where he nodded to the security guard before walking to the lift which would take him to the fourth floor. His office was in the nicest of the half a dozen Ministry offices in central London which were now occupied by the many, many bureaucrats required to interpret London's eccentric laws.

When things had started to go a bit crazy and security was at its height, people in London had grizzled and complained. There had been talk of rebellion and several unsuccessful uprisings. Everyone had been unhappy and so someone, some government advisor, had come up with the idea of devising a written constitution: by the people for the people. Brilliant. Except that the people who self-selected themselves for such tasks were not necessarily suited to them. The particular group of people who took on the role of writing the constitution turned out to be made up of idealists, imbeciles, anarchists and practical jokers. At least the nihilists hadn't got involved – although that was only because they couldn't be bothered. Each of the members of the committee tasked with writing the constitution had had an equal vote on what it should contain. Lucas didn't like living in a dictatorship, as he did now, but he could see how democracy could be a bit of a burden when you were expected to obey the will of the people and the people turned out to be such a bunch of fools.

On the fourth floor, as Lucas walked down the long corridor towards his office, each brass plaque on each doorway he passed told something about the way London now functioned: Inspector of Cats, Inspector of Hedgerows & Grass Verges, Inspector of Inventions & Gadgets, Inspector of Women & Family Relationships. The departments ranged from the esoteric to the worthy to the downright silly and as he passed the fourth floor toilets, Lucas was amused to recall hearing that the reason there were two sets on every floor, one with urinals, one without, was because women had once been allocated toilets in every office in London; it seemed ludicrous. There was now a whole department tasked with agreeing what it meant to work outside the home – whether it was OK, for example, for women to work in other women's homes or whether they were to be restricted to working in their own homes. There were all sorts of exceptions and loopholes which had to be debated, refined and then policed. It ought to have been easy to sort out but it wasn't so straightforward once they got into the detail, especially as there were so many amateurs at senior level, appointed because of nepotism and favouritism, and because so many competent civil servants had been imprisoned as suspected terrorists or paedophiles or, occasionally, both. What about the homes of relatives? And what was a home, exactly? A family-owned restaurant, a nursing home, a children's home? Was any one of these a home as set out in the constitution?

Last stop before Lucas's office was the Inspector of Women's Travel. It seemed as if every woman in London claimed somehow to be related to every other woman. It was the job of poor old Fielding next door to Lucas to keep track of which family relationships between women had been confirmed so that their visits to each other could be officially sanctioned. There was such a backlog that women criss-crossed all over London unofficially anyway, pending review of their cases. Men made the laws. Women set out to exploit the loopholes in them.

Finally Lucas reached the door to his office with its polished plaque proclaiming him Inspector of Miracles. He was still rather proud of the job, though a lot of it boiled down to sifting information. None of the other countries, principalities, nation states and sundry territories around the world had an Inspector of Miracles, so far as he knew. It might have been a way of incentivising him but he had been told that they watched his progress abroad with interest. If he should ever turn up evidence of a bona fide miracle, they'd surely want to renegotiate trade treaties and open a political dialogue with London.

Did anyone really expect him to uncover a miracle? He didn't expect it himself. But the right to believe in miracles was enshrined in the constitution. And if a miracle is to be believed in collectively, then first it has to be found, next it has to be validated and finally it has to be presented to the people of London – and then the world – so that they can believe in it. All of this fell under his remit. It was a lot of work and potentially rather interesting despite the sifting, and it was why others were sometimes jealous of him.

'What you up to, mate?'

He looked up to see Jones in the doorway and recoiled slightly. Jones was Head of Security and known to spy on his wife. You could go into his office to borrow a paperclip and get an eyeful of Joanna Jones in the shower, one of her pink nipples displayed in close-up on Jones's computer screen like a small, sightless creature quenching its thirst in the rain.

'Another face of the Virgin Mary in a flan. I've got to go to Earl's Court this afternoon.'

'Will you declare a miracle if it looks like the Virgin Mary?'

'You know what, Jones? It would be a miracle if it didn't, the trouble they go to, arranging the bits of leek and onion and all the rest of it into the shape of a face.'

Jones laughed at that one. Men found him funny. Jones laughed for just one second too long, in a slightly fawning way – though he might have been mocking him.

'Why do they do it, if they know you'll catch them out?'

'They're lonely, the women. I think they're glad of the attention, some of them.'

'You ever get reports from men that they've found a miracle?'

'Yeah, course. I hear from all sorts, right across the board: every race, every class, every religion. But it's predominantly women.'

'And they ever, er, they ever come on to you? You know? They ever answer the door in their nightie and...'

'No.'

'No. I didn't think so. You never know.'

'Well, your wife wouldn't and nor would mine.'

'Honestly, mate. I don't know about Joanna.'

Lucas shuffled some papers, to let Jones know that he was busy. But Jones didn't want to leave. He said, 'Have you heard? There's something going on.'

'With Joanna?'

'No. Troops on the move, prisoners coming in. I think we're in for a bit of trouble.'

'The only ones who'd want to do anything about it are the women – wives, sisters, mothers, daughters of the men who get taken away, and they've never succeeded in getting a man released from prison. They can't even protest legally since the Richmond gathering was quashed. That wasn't anything to do with you, Jones? It was pretty brutal.'

'Let's be realistic – it's the clamp-down on miscreants that ensures the continuing prosperity of this fair city.'

'Because they're terrorists?'

'Because their assets are confiscated and never returned.'

'If they bring in more prisoners, where will they put them? The camps?'

'Camps? What have you heard about camps?'

'Secret long-term prison camps where they stay so long that half the inmates become feminised. And they run on treadmills all day to keep London's electricity going.'

'Hahaha. Hahaha. That's a new one. Very energy efficient. Might suggest it at the next council meeting. What else have you heard?'

'Torture. Executions underground; the cremated remains of the prisoners thrown into the rivers that flow under the city and carried out to the sea so they can never be identified.'

'Just keep your nose clean. You don't ever want to find out what they do.'

'Yeah, OK.'

'You need to think about Angela.' Jones seemed anxious. That was odd. 'They're talking about rounding them up for their own good.'

'The wives?'

'Yes.'

'Where would they put them?'

'Let's hope it's just talk.'

'They'd put them in a detention centre somewhere and we'd have to queue up outside just to fuck them? You wonder what it would take to get this place back on track.'

'I know damn well what it would take,' said Jones.

Lucas didn't. He looked at Jones and saw his eyes were glittering.

'Mate, it would take a bloody miracle.'

3 Joanna Jones

He couldn't have said why he went to the house to see Joanna Jones. It was on a whim. There was no specific train of thought in which he'd said to himself, 'I won't go out inspecting miracles today, I won't pop home and surprise Angela, my wife and the woman I love; instead, I'll go and see Joanna Jones and risk ruining the rest of my life.' If Jones found out, he would have him arrested. He would visit him in an underground prison and stare down at him through the bars in the cage and piss on him. For what? Whatever he was going to do now – and actually he still had no idea what it was – it had better be good. He told himself he just wanted to understand Angela by getting to know Joanna, by comparing the two women.

He sat in his car, parked a little way down the street from where Jones lived. He watched a man sweeping the street. He watched men delivering food and other provisions to the houses along the streets, the housewives coming to the door, chatting a little longer than necessary to the delivery men, glad of the company.

He watched a woman come out of Jones's house – not Joanna, a heavier-set woman, probably older. She crossed the road, head down, face covered by her veil, arms at her sides, a coal scuttle with legs, her comedy walk necessitated by the long, restrictive outer garment covering her clothes. As she passed by his car, he wound the window down.

'Ma'am?'

She looked terrified.

'I want to talk to you, ma'am. Stay where you are.'

She peered at him but said nothing. He took his Ministry badge from the inside pocket of his suit jacket, flipped it open and dangled it out of the window so she could see it. There was really no need, she'd have deduced that he was somewhere near the top of the hierarchy because of the car. 'How do you know Mrs Jones?'

'She's a relative of mine.' No kidding. But he wasn't interested in calling her on that. If he pricked the finger of every dissembling woman with the blood test kit he and every other high-ranking Ministry employee had been issued with and sent the sample off to the records office for analysis, he wouldn't have a moment to spare for any other work. He didn't care about the database, he didn't care about their DNA. They all had an X chromosome, that was enough for him. Let them have their visits. Poor cows.

'What's in the basket?'

'Nothing. Just...I brought her a jar of my home-made jam.'

'Looks kind of uneven-shaped. What else you got?'

'I keep my knitting in there, too. Making a little cloche hat for my granddaughter. Would you like a jar of jam, sir? I've some to spare.'

'I need to speak to her. It's important. Go back in and tell her to come out here.'

The woman stared at him.

'It's important. We haven't got much time. Go on. Oh, and listen to me, old woman, breathe a word of this to anyone and you're in just as much trouble as she is.'

The woman wasn't even that old, maybe forty-five. What could she do? She went to fetch Joanna and presently she appeared, covered up. Joanna crossed the street to his car. Her friend stayed on the other side of the road, watching. Lucas waved her off and she had no choice but to comply. He watched her in the rear-view mirror until she disappeared from view. Joanna came up to the driver's side of the car and peered in at him.

'Get in,' he said, and she did. He wound up the window and locked the car doors. They were safe from any intrusion; a little oasis of officialdom in her suburban street. Even a soldier would no more come up and knock on the window than take out his automatic rifle and shoot himself in the foot. Lucas was protected because of who he was. It was only then that he realised why he had come here. She had a little freckle on her left nipple. She had a plump bottom and tiny stretch-marks on her thighs, like shirring elastic. He had seen her lick toast crumbs from a breakfast plate in the privacy of her own home, when she thought no one was watching her.

'Do you know why I'm here?'

'No.' She looked uncomfortable. She looked guilty about something. Maybe she'd been having secret meetings about how to overthrow the government under the guise of talking about jam and knitting. One thing that had always worked in Lucas's favour was his long silences. He was daydreaming, usually, but it always seemed to other people as if he was holding his nerve. They caved and tried to fill the silence. Joanna was no different. 'What do you want?'

'Do you trust your husband?'

'What?'

He could rummage around under the ugly black material that covered her, push her skirt off, get her knickers off. He could kiss her. Would she close her eyes and lie back, like Angela did? Would she feel inside his trousers? Would she turn around and shuffle her plump bottom back towards him? The car was a luxury model but still a bit cramped for that sort of thing. If she wanted to avoid banging her head on the roof, she'd have to keep her head tilted forward in a 'yes', signalling agreement with something or other for a protracted length of time. Would he have to talk dirty to her? Maybe he'd say something about covering her with jam and licking it off.

The black material she was wearing was voluminous and it would be difficult getting his hands inside it. If he ruched it up, as if he was an assistant on the haberdashery counter at a large department store, she might start laughing. Or she might fight him off. He was sure she'd enjoy it, if he had sex with her. He just wasn't sure how to get to that point from where they were just now, sitting in his car with her staring at him through the peephole in her veil in frank astonishment.

'Would you do something for me, if you thought it might help your husband?'

Her eyes widened. When that's all you had to look at, it meant that a woman couldn't hide what she was feeling. If she was wearing ordinary clothes, you'd be looking at her tits. But here it was, an honest, if enforced, communication.

'It's not a test,' he said.

As soon as he said it, she thought it was a test. 'Did he send you?'

'What do you think?'

She didn't know. She didn't know what to think. She couldn't follow the logic of what he was doing. No surprise as there was no logic.

He unbuttoned the veil across her face. He looked at her. He wanted to kiss her. He wanted to put his tongue in her mouth – that funny tumbling of something warm and soft and alive, like interrupting a clothes dryer mid-cycle and reaching into it to rescue a kitten. The next step might have been to touch her.

He didn't kiss her. He didn't touch her. He said, 'I didn't come here to spy on you for him.'

'I can't do anything dangerous. I'm not brave. You know? I'm sorry, if you're trying to help me. Don't ask me to do anything.'

'When you leave the house, where do you go?'

'I go to the women's groups.'

'If I leave a message for you, will you meet me one day?'

'I don't know. I'm not sure if it's a good idea.'

He unlocked the car doors. She buttoned up her veil. He didn't want to meet her 'one day'. He wanted to take her to a hotel room now. If he asked her to do it, would she?

'Why does he spy on you?'

'Jonathan? He's worried about me.'

But then he saw the change in her eyes. She knew – she suddenly knew why he had come; it was because he'd seen her. She knew. He was frightened of her. But he wanted to go to Jones's office and look and see if she did anything differently tomorrow, knowing he might be watching.

She got out of the car. She walked across the road to the door of her house. She went inside. He never saw her again.

4   The Letters

Angela didn't think it was prying to look at the journal. Jesmond had wanted Lucas to see it, after all. She thought of herself as his proxy. There was no way Lucas was going to read anything left for him by that man. Besides, it was rare that something so interesting happened to her. Jesmond had given her a journal, full of scrappy ideas for poems, mundane thoughts, little jokes. And a dozen letters, handwritten on thin sheets of paper, each one sent, opened and then returned to him in the envelope it had been sent in. It wasn't much of a life but it was a life – and it was hers to peruse.

Much as she tried to pretend to herself that she was doing this for Lucas, she had to acknowledge that she saw it as a form of entertainment. She felt guilty but it was such a lovely thing to have in her possession. Reading it would be like having a friend dropping by to gossip. She had precious few distractions apart from visits from a few women 'relatives'.

The letters in the journal were written to a woman. Angela ascertained that much when she flicked through the first couple of them, quickly, trying not to read or take in any of the information and risk spoiling the treat.

She opened a letter at random and began to read:

> Until I met you, I thought there was something scientific about love, and the key to it was getting the balance just right in the mixture of sex and companionship. I thought loving someone involved knowing what vegetables the other person liked and whether or not they'd enjoy the film I was watching. In other words, I thought it was a bit boring, apart from the sex. But you make all of it disconcerting and exciting. I love you so much.

She decided to save the letters. She would open them one at a time and in order; savour them, like instalments in a soap opera.

She looked at the dates on the envelopes, trying to match the day or the date of the letters to the entries in Jesmond's journal. But often there was nothing in the journal, or nothing that seemed relevant. Perhaps his private thoughts weren't suitable for 'the archive' and he'd concealed them, coded them or destroyed them.

She opened the first letter. There were no others tucked into the journal that came before it, chronologically. But reading it, it was obvious she was joining the party some time after it had started.

Darling,

I read a new poem at a gig last night: 'Spoiled'. I wrote it for you. It's an apology for spoiling everything by remarking that I had spoiled everything after making love to you. That night with you was the happiest of my life. I wish I had said as much to you. But I had worshipped you for so long, I was frightened. I said, 'I've spoiled you.' Do you remember?

When I read the new poem last night, I think the audience were surprised at the tenderness expressed in it. But after a short silence, they whooped and clapped appreciatively enough. Some called for more. And the funny thing is that when I talked to them about it afterwards, it turned out that they all thought – every single one of them – that the 'you' I addressed in the poem, my longed-for love, the one I felt I had insulted with my desire, with my crass murmurings, it was England! Yes, I can write anything, any self-flagellating piece in which I offer to crush up the splinters of my heart and put them on the ground and walk over them to prove my love, and these people will assume I'm talking about the revolution.

You've teased me in the past, saying I think it's all about me. And it is one of my failings, I admit. Everything, even the way I relate to you, is about me. (Although I don't know who else I should channel my feelings through. If 'you and me' can't be about how I feel about you, then I'm stumped. I don't want to love you through another man – but that's too damn close to our current situation to joke about.) Anyway, what's so refreshing about these fucking audiences is they listen to my stuff, my carefully-wrought, delicately-crafted, heart-splintering stuff, and they think it's all about them. Ha ha ha. Be careful what you wish for, eh, my darling? Oh, I know. I said something along those lines to you that night. But I didn't mean it to come out quite how it did. You see, I had been wishing for it for so long. For so long. The world has changed, because of you.

p.s. Some members of the audience seemed to think the word in the poem was 'soiled'. You didn't think I said soiled, did you? No wonder you were cross.

J. xx

5 Atlantis

The first thing Lucas realised when he saw Angela that evening was that he couldn't have sex with her if he was likely to think about Joanna Jones because that would be disrespectful and almost as bad as cheating on her. The second thing he realised was that he didn't want to have sex with Angela anyway because he now suspected she only did it to pass the time, and he was angry about that, and this anger had perhaps motivated his almost suicidally imprudent visit to the Jones household.

The third thing he realised was that he had changed since this morning and Angela hadn't. She was just the same lovely woman she had always been. But he was behaving as if she was the one who had changed.

He went to the cupboard and looked at the jars arranged on the shelves. He was looking for jam. He wanted to know if Angela was in any way similar to Joanna Jones. He wanted to know if she was the sort of woman who would sit with a stranger in a car, and if she might then go to a hotel room with him for sex, if she thought her life or her husband's life somehow depended on it. And if so, he wanted to blame her for it, rather than himself. Ultimately, of course, society was to blame: confining women to their homes, taking away their right to work, to protest. In recent months, he had sometimes congratulated himself for not beating Angela or abusing her, as other men did with their wives. He realised – what number was he up to? Was that number four or five? He also realised that it was not enough. It was not right. They had to get out of London. They had not a moment to lose. It didn't help that Jones would be home by now, would have spoken to his wife, might already be on to him. Why add that danger in to the mix, as if the stakes were not already high enough? Perhaps he had behaved incautiously so they would have no choice but to leave London?

He wanted Angela to have children. He wanted to live in Cornwall with her and the children. If not Cornwall, then Wales. If he thought there was any chance of getting there, he'd build a boat and sail them to Australia. It was so remote and such a dreamed-of paradise, Australia. You might as well talk about the Lost City of Atlantis. It seemed unimaginable that there was once air travel, freely available to all. You turned up at an airport, climbed aboard a plane, strapped yourself in and in a few hours you were there, all the way at the other side of the world, where you could explore and wander at will. Now, the paperwork alone would take longer than the flight. But anyway, there were no flights to be had because of terrorism.

There were still ships, trains, cars. But few countries allowed visitors by those routes because of what they might bring: terrorism, disease, unpleasant ideas. He imagined going to Australia and inadvertently infecting that beautiful, happy, liberal country with his ideas. He imagined somehow managing to get on to a ship and arriving in Australia and then spoiling it all by doing to a woman what he had wanted to do to Joanna Jones. He had behaved despicably. He had frightened her.

'Lucas? What are you looking for in there? You want something to eat?'

Maybe Angela was frightened of him. She was worried because he was looking in the cupboard and she thought he couldn't find the Marmite or something. Maybe she didn't have sex with him to pass the time. She had sex with him because he was her husband and she was frightened of him. She did it to please him. She did it because when the women sat around in the women's groups and talked about what life was like, she realised that other women's husbands beat them. She did it not because he had blue eyes and she fancied him rotten, nor even because she was bored and she wanted to pass the time. She did it because she was frightened of him.

'Lucas? Should I cook you something?'

'Don't you want to be something more than a housewife, cooking for me?'

She was hurt by that, though she tried not to let him see it. He'd assumed that men were more intelligent than women but then he'd never been forced by law to sit around the house all day waiting for something to happen. If the incarceration didn't make you stupid, it would certainly make you cautious. You wouldn't want to reveal that you knew anything. You wouldn't want to invite criticism or do anything that would invite a beating. Maybe women just seemed stupid. He had hurt two women in one day and it made him feel guilty and depressed.

She said, 'You want to go upstairs? Let's go up and have a cuddle.'

'I'll have a shower. I'll be up later, OK?'

Was that the first time he'd ever turned her down? He couldn't remember another time. He went into the bathroom. He took off his clothes, he ran the water. He soaped all over his body. He washed his hair with the shampoo. He conditioned his hair. He thought about Joanna Jones bending over, water running down over her plump little bottom and dripping down her thighs. He thought about all the various possibilities that would be available to him if she were here now, blushing and bending over. He washed himself off with the soap and then he turned the shower water to cold for the last half a minute.

He went into the bedroom in his towel. Angela was lying on the bed reading something. She closed it and tucked it under the bed as he came in. He hadn't known she kept a journal. Not that he minded.

She was in her dressing gown with nothing underneath. She turned to look at him. She smiled at him.

'You look better,' she said.

'You don't look so bad yourself.'

He threw the towel on the floor and jumped on her. She was warm and his skin was cold. She shivered and giggled and grabbed hold of him. He made love to her. He realised how much he loved her. He told her, over and over, 'I love you, Angela.' He really meant it. She meant everything to him.

Afterwards he heated up a pizza and made them a salad and they shared a bottle of wine and they lay in bed and watched TV – one of those nature programmes Angela liked because she said it made her glad she wasn't a puma or a lion, having to struggle just to survive.

6 Spoiled

Reading Jesmond's letters was strangely intimate. It was flattering to have this famous man addressing her directly, talking of love, parties, infidelity, the genesis of his poetry, even though, of course, he wasn't addressing her; he had written the letters to someone else. She was growing very fond of him. She was falling for him, she might have said, if she wasn't already married. She had never had an insight into the mind of a grown-up in this way. She'd never talked to her own father as an adult because by the time she had grown up he had been taken away. She was struck, over and over again, by how like her generation Jesmond's generation was, and also how different; less guarded but more damaged. Needier, somehow, but less defensive. She knew she couldn't assess a whole generation based on a few scribbles and rejected love letters from a man like Jesmond. And yet still, she did.

She wished she could share this with Lucas, talk over Jesmond's motivations, speculate about who this woman was, who he was writing to. When he came to the house, hadn't Jesmond said something about collecting shells on a beach with a woman he was in love with? Surely that was the same woman. Unfortunately Angela didn't remember him saying her name.

She couldn't talk to Lucas about it. He'd only say, 'I don't know how he could live that god-awful, bohemian lifestyle that he and my father lived, caught up in the importance of their music and their poetry and their feelings, and shagging around while the country went down the shitter.' Something like that, anyway. It was a pretty fair summary of his opinion of Jesmond.

It was illogical but as Angela read Jesmond's letters, it felt as if he had known that she would one day read them and that (even though she had only just been born at the time of writing) he was in some sense writing to her future self. If so, she was sure he would have been disappointed if he'd discovered what she was really like. The letters assumed a wisdom and complexity in the reader, a level of sophistication that she didn't have. She had barely travelled further than the edge of the kitchen table, and the reader of the letters – the legitimate reader – seemed to have seen and done so much. She wished she could have some experiences that would change her. She longed to see something of the rest of the world and learn from what she saw. If Jesmond had been there to talk it through with her, would he have cautioned her to be careful what she wished for? Or would he have joked with her about it, as he used to joke with the woman he loved?

Angela had looked in the journal and found a scrap of the poem Jesmond had mentioned in the first letter she had read. It had been written hastily, without revisions, as if it was a first draft, and then there was a single line going through it, diagonally, from bottom left to top right, as if he wasn't happy with it. But he hadn't ripped the page out or scribbled through the words completely, as he had elsewhere in the book.

Spoiled
My touch left a muddy
fingerprint, a speck on the film stock,
a smear on the family china,
a fly in the marmalade you
were making.
Don't reproach me.
Don't think I'm trying to
trivialise by mentioning
household items. I wish we had
a household.
I wish we were together,
you and me.

I would take care of you.
I would not breathe on you or
touch you or handle you – there I
go again, saying the wrong thing.
I mean I would find a way to
worship you, to be with you
without changing you while still
knowing that to be with you would
change me.

She couldn't have read it to Lucas. He hated poetry. 'What's the point?' he'd ask. 'What's it good for? What can it do?'

She'd leave it to educated people (the archivists?) to judge whether or not it was any good. Lucas would sneer at that business about the fly in the marmalade. Surely it didn't matter – all poetry, pretty much by definition, was actually rather trying to read, especially when it had been written to be performed, as Jesmond's was. Reading it was a test of faith, somehow. But it could change people – she believed that. At any rate, reading this had changed her. It made her want to be the sort of woman who could inspire a man to write poetry. It made her want to be interesting. As things stood, no one would ever want to write about her, no matter how kind she tried to be, or how eager to please. In fact, from her rudimentary reading of the relevant literary works (or rather, the summaries of classic novels that she had found in encyclopaedias), the kinder and the more eager the woman, the less likely she was to inspire poetry.

She wished she had talked to Jesmond when he'd visited. She'd come to think of him as a pompous, vain drunk who troubled her husband – because that's what Lucas thought. And although she'd felt sorry for him because of the life he led, she'd never tried to make a connection with him.

Never mind. She would make an effort next time he dropped round.

7 Christina

The next day, Lucas had to go and inspect a miracle. He decided to get it over with and go straight there rather than stopping in to the office first. He didn't like doing the home visits. It could be so embarrassing. There'd be the walk up to the front door, where he'd find himself making a judgement about the people inside before he even set eyes on them. Then there'd be the particular smell of the house; something acrid and left over. Then there'd be the people themselves; the desperation, the smallness of them compared with their big dreams.

When he started out in this job, he'd assumed it would be mostly religious establishments that would contact him. But it wasn't. Perhaps such places had their own rigorous tests to which they subjected potential miracles before reporting them. Or perhaps they had miracles and they kept them to themselves, storing them up to store up power which they would unleash one day, when the time came – whenever that might be. Then again, perhaps miracles didn't happen in churches, mosques and temples because God does not exist and miracles do not exist. It seemed entirely feasible to him that these places were there simply to guard that secret. But try telling ordinary people that God does not exist. They weren't interested. They wanted to believe in something.

It was funny but he did think, as he set off for work that morning, how brilliant it would be if he found a miracle. He would tell Angela. It would be their passport to Cornwall. He would have sex with her from every angle and never think about Joanna Jones. And then he thought how strange it was that if you tried not to think about someone, their name popped into your mind, like that.

Trying not to think of Joanna didn't work so he'd have to keep himself busy with other things, putting time and distance between them and simply not thinking of her for months on end, until he never thought of her. But for now, he was wondering if she was at home wondering if he was watching her. He'd like to go into Jones's office and have a quick peek, just to make sure, but he was in the car en route to a reported miracle, so he couldn't. The thought of her began take him over. He'd have to give himself over to it for now and then just try to remember not to try not to think about her in future.

But for now, well, she would be standing in the kitchen in a T-shirt and a little pair of frilly knickers. She would have jam on her fingers. She would look up at one of the cameras Jones had positioned around the place. She would bring her fingers up to her mouth and put the middle three fingers in her mouth up to the first set of knuckles, then she would lick each of her fingers all the way up and down, one by one. She would look at the camera and her expression, close up, would be exactly the same as the expression he had seen in her eyes in the slot made by her veil.

She would go upstairs… He decided to pull in for a moment, to a layby, under the pretext of consulting a map. No one could see in through the tinted windows but it wasn't a good idea to drive while he was feeling like this. It wasn't safe. He didn't want to have a crash and hurt someone or himself. He didn't want it reported in the news that came in on the computer in Jones's office, 'man with erection kills widow and children,' or, 'man dies in car crash, with erection.' They didn't report details like that, of course. Or he had never seen them reported. Perhaps it had never happened before? No, men had dirty thoughts about other men's wives all the time.

He imagined Joanna Jones going upstairs, knowing the camera was watching her. Knowing her husband was watching her and had perhaps noticed a difference in the way she was behaving. Would she find it stimulating to think that her husband was jealous and had only himself to blame? Would Jones find it stimulating? No, that wasn't an image he wanted to pursue; Jones wanking in the men's lavatory at the thought of other men looking at his wife.

Joanna Jones would go upstairs to the bathroom and remove her knickers. Perhaps she would take a razor and shave the backs of her legs at the top. She might not know that he would find that erotic, so perhaps she would not. What had he told her? What would she do so that he would know that it was for him?

Had he mentioned jam? Possibly not. He had certainly mentioned her husband. He had hinted at danger. He had thought of having sex with her but not said it aloud. That was all their relationship consisted of. And, to be fair, to many minds it wouldn't quite constitute a relationship.

It was a warm, sunny day and he had the air conditioning turned up in the car. Still, he was perspiring. He felt guilty. He wondered whether Angela had fantasies about other men. Thank God women weren't allowed out of the house. He didn't mean that, of course. But still. Who did she come into contact with? The delivery drivers, the postman, the milkman. Neighbours going off to work in the morning. Did she have salacious thoughts about any of them? If he asked her tonight, would it put an idea into her mind that had never been there? If he asked her, would she think it was a fantasy of his and try to please him by naming someone? Would she turn to him with her dressing down half open and nothing underneath and say yes, when I touch myself, I think of Jones. Fortunately not – she didn't know Jones.

If Jones asked Joanna, would she tell him that she thought of the man from the Ministry and describe Lucas? Not if she had any sense. He thought of Jones slapping Joanna, saying something like, 'I'll beat you black and blue, mate.' Did Jones call his wife 'mate'? He didn't want to think about Jones. He felt aggrieved, as if Jones was deliberately intruding on his fantasy.

He drove to the address he had been given and parked his car outside. He walked up to the front door. He saw a few weeds in the path. He saw evidence of peeling paint. He saw a sweet wrapper on the ground, left behind by the bin men. He didn't stoop to pick it up; it would blow away soon enough.

The miracle that had been reported was something to do with a child. So many women seemed to have a fantasy of themselves as a Mary figure, with their child a saint. It would make their lives easier to bear, no doubt, to have a child who would be looked after and revered. Perhaps the women thought they would be taken away with the child to live in a palace somewhere and be protected. His own belief was that even if he made a report to say that he had found a miracle, someone would intervene, take the people concerned into custody for questioning, harass them, accuse them of being involved in terrorism, then lock them up somewhere for good. Or terminate them. Maybe it was just as well he'd never had to report anything as a miracle – yet.

The woman who answered the door seemed nice enough, if a little careworn. Her name was Maureen and she was old enough to be his mum. She invited him in. He didn't have any erotic thoughts, other than to note that he wasn't having erotic thoughts, which immediately conjured up an image of Joanna Jones in a pair of frilly pants with a pot of jam in her hand, an image he was fortunately able to put aside almost immediately.

Maureen took him in to the front room and offered him a cup of tea. He said yes, so that she'd have to go away to the kitchen to make it and he could sit quietly and look around. There were no religious artefacts around the place, no pictures of Jesus. It wasn't against the law to practice religion, although there weren't many men who wanted to become priests any more. It was often taken as a confession of paedophilia and priests could expect a lot of interest from the authorities. Most took lovers, or pretended to do so, installing attractive female housekeepers to ensure they were not mistaken for paedophiles by the local community.

'Have they told you anything?' Maureen asked.

'No.' He always said that, of course. He let them put it into their own words.

She droned on. He was feeling unerotic now and back on track. Perhaps he had been under some sort of stress that had now gone away. If he had been a woman, he'd have said it was hormonal. There must have been something, some extraneous thing, that had caused him to behave so oddly. Perhaps he had been the subject of a test? Perhaps Jones had come into his office yesterday and sprayed an undetectable hormone around to gauge its effect on him. Jones was a brute, unpredictable and coarse. Lucas could hardly bear being in the same office building some days. He didn't know how he endured it. He became sentimental. He told himself that he didn't care what he had to endure, just so long as he could protect Angela. Just so long as she loved him and she didn't ever betray him or subject him to any kind of test. He loved her and he was going to prove it by taking her away to Cornwall.

Maureen was looking at him. He looked back at her, calmly.

'So what do you think?' said Maureen.

'I can't really say.'

'Well, what should I do?'

'Who else have you told?'

'Well, as I was saying…'

He had drifted off and she wasn't impressed. But the thing was, he wasn't here to impress her. It was she who had to try to impress him.

'Did you want to take notes?'

'No.'

He had a piece of the lemon drizzle cake she offered him. It was home-made. He sat and thought about his options while he ate it. He wondered, if this was that rare and impossible thing, a real miracle, ought he to take the woman hostage? He wouldn't hurt her of course. He'd put a gun to her head for the benefit of any security forces who might turn up to rescue her and he'd call for Angela to join him. He'd state his demands: safe passage to Cornwall.

It would never happen. They'd never let him go. They'd blow him and Maureen and Angela to high heaven, miracle or not. In fact, if it was a real miracle, it would save the authorities the job of deciding what to do about it, if the evidence was destroyed in the process of protecting lives and the safety of the citizens of London.

What about Australia? If he could get a message to someone in Australia that he had found a miracle, would someone from there come and save him? Probably not.

Even if people in Australia believed in miracles, they wouldn't sanction hostage-taking, wouldn't care if a person such as he should live or die. They wouldn't want to give sanctuary to a gun-wielding, adulterous-leaning miracle inspector. Besides, he didn't have a gun.

'So do you want to see her?'

'Who?'

'Christina. Do you want to see her? She's next door.'

'Might as well.'

He stood and smiled brightly. Poor old Maureen. What a life.

Christina was lying on top of the covers on a single bed in the next room. She was an unremarkable-looking child, as they so often were. She looked about five years old although she might have been older. Maureen had probably mentioned her age but there was no need to get mired in details.

He went up to Christina and smiled at her. 'Hello.' No response from Christina. He tried again. 'Hello, Christine.'

'Christina.'

'What?'

'Christina, not Christine.'

'Oh, I see.'

'She understands you.'

'Yes. Does she speak?'

'The doctor says there's nothing actually wrong with her vocal chords.'

He hadn't been paying attention. What was the miracle, exactly? That this poor little child was alive? That

48

she could understand? Or was she supposed to heal the sick? Some of them were very good at the piano but he couldn't see one in the room, so he might escape hearing any Rachmaninoff today. Dare he ask Maureen to go through it again? What if she reported him? But she wouldn't. Who would she report him to?

Lucas said, 'You want to leave me alone with Christina, here? Might help me get a feel for her… special qualities.'

She didn't. He suddenly saw in her face all the awful fears every mother had these days. Maureen thought that he might do something nasty to little Christina. She didn't believe that he would do it but she thought it. She'd been trained to think it. They all had. Even he thought it. He thought that if a man was left alone with little Christina, he might start touching her inappropriately. He himself wouldn't do it. The next man wouldn't do it, nor the next man, nor the next. You'd have to search long and hard to find one who would. But the suggestion was enough to condemn them all to this hell of a life. There was no proper education for the kids, no life outside the home for the women, all of it to keep them safe from inappropriate touching. What if the thought of it was more harmful? What if the fear that covered them all was worse than one child sometimes being touched? You couldn't say it, of course. Say something like that and they'd lock you up forever. Besides, he wasn't sure if he even really meant it. He wasn't sure what he thought about anything. They'd all been conditioned to believe what the authorities wanted them to believe.

'Sir? Do you mind if I stay with her? In case she needs something?'

'No, course not. It's better if you stay. I'm just going to talk to her. Or perhaps I could watch for a minute, while you talk to her. Could you talk to her?'

Maureen looked relieved. She'd decided he was a decent bloke. She'd probably decided that the moment he'd had a piece of her lemon drizzle cake. She'd have made it specially for his visit and another man – someone like Jones – wouldn't have accepted it. Someone like Jones might have wanted it but he'd have said no. Whereas Lucas knew she'd gone to a lot of trouble and he'd had a piece and it was quite nice. He wasn't born this way, with the ability to put himself in someone else's place; to empathise. It was the sort of thing you picked up, doing a job like this.

'Do you have kids?'

'Not yet. One day.'

'Married, though? Young chap like you, handsome.'

Alright, Maureen, calm down. I had a piece of your lemon drizzle cake, that's all. 'Can you talk to Christina, then, tell her why I've come?'

Maureen turned to her little daughter. 'He's heard you're special, Christina.'

That caught him unexpectedly, nearly choked him. Everything about it. The love in Maureen's voice when she spoke to the child. The lie of it, the terrible lie in that word special. She was a sweet enough little child, she was loved. But special? She was terribly unfortunate; that was the word he would have used. He felt suddenly so

50

desolate and desperate that if he'd had a gun in his hand now, he would have put the barrel in his mouth and pulled the trigger. Perhaps he'd even do the kid the favour of taking her with him. Perhaps he'd lean down and put his head against her little head with its soft shiny hair and put this imaginary gun against his temple and blow them both away.

'See, that's what she does when she's happy. See that? That little smile? It takes a tremendous amount of effort for Christina to do that. She only does that for people she knows, or if she likes you.'

'Lovely.' He ought to – but he thought of it quite often and he couldn't do it for everybody and so in fact he had never done it – he ought to remember their address and send them some money anonymously. Do something to help them, make their lives better.

'Oh, but that isn't the miracle.'

'Of course not. No.'

'You see, if you had something – if you were unhappy…'

'What d'you mean?'

'If you were unhappy about something. Or if you were sick. I mean – I know you're not…of course. But if you were troubled or…'

'Oh, I get it. Like a cat?'

He meant it genuinely. Any warm-bodied, empathetic creature without the power of speech: the perfect confessor. Always listening, never giving advice. Poor old Maureen, he might as well have slapped her. He might as well have dragged her by the hair into the kitchen, filled the sink with water on top of – he hadn't seen it, he was guessing here – its dirty dishes, and repeatedly dunked her face in it, pushing her head down towards the plates with (guessing again) their traces of baked bean juice, then held it under the water as a very few uneaten baked beans dislodged from the plate and floated slowly towards the surface, like lilies unfurling in the daylight.

'I wouldn't say that, sir.'

'No.'

'It's altruistic, isn't it? A miracle. They never try to heal themselves. It's others they help.'

'No, exactly. Standard question. Right answer.'

'You're not writing any of this down?'

'I'll make the report after, don't worry. I like to take it all in. You've got your head bent over a piece of paper, you're likely to miss something. The sly look between conspirators.'

'Oh.'

'Or the moment when the miracle happens. You see what I mean?'

'Oh. Yes. '

She was reappraising him, Maureen. His stock was rising. He was in charge, he knew what he was doing. She'd thought him a bit of an idiot; too young, with his blue eyes and his pretty face and his day-dreaming. Now she knew he was in charge. And she thought that because she could see that he was clever, it made her clever. But she could only see it because he let her see.

He turned to the child. 'Now then, Christina.'

What on earth was he going to say to her? To be fair, he did think he could see a tiny little change in her expression, a glimmer.

'She likes you.'

'Yes.'

They sat in silence for a while, all three of them, Maureen content now for him to be in charge. He wondered whether he ought to go through some farcical examination whereby he brought in the sick and the heartsick and paraded them in front of Christina to see whether they could be cured. But it didn't seem fair on the kid, to raise her hopes only to say it hadn't worked. Maureen might quite like the company but she didn't have money to be spending on lemon drizzle cake for sundry visitors. Besides, she'd be bitterly disappointed when he declared there hadn't been a miracle.

'Does she like singing?'

'Yes.'

'My wife has a lovely voice.'

'Yes?'

'Angela.'

'Really? I'd love to hear her sing some time. I'm sure Christina…'

'Ah, well. She rarely gets outside the house.' That's the way you expressed it these days, as if it was a minor, temporary inconvenience, particular to the person being discussed. You'd never say, 'Isn't it terrible, all the women in London being under house arrest?'

'Did you ever work, Maureen, outside the home?'

She looked a bit nervous. You ever asked anyone a personal question, they assumed it was a trap. Quite right, too. But Maureen was game. She wanted him to declare that Christina was a miracle. So pretty much anything he said, she was going to play along. He thought she was going to say she had done something domestic and dreary. But she didn't.

'I used to read the news. On the local network.' Christ! Now he was interested. 'It might have led to something. I was only young. I actually reported on the attacks that changed everything – though I didn't know how far-reaching the effects were going to be at the time.'

'No one did.'

'I had Christina very late.'

'Yes. Or rather, I mean, you don't look…'

She laughed. 'I know what you mean.'

He realised that something had changed. He was talking to her as an equal. At first, he'd dismissed her as some worried old bag with a disabled daughter who couldn't come to terms with what had happened to the child. But her situation was more complex than that. Here was a woman who had worked for a living, who'd once had a job. He was being awkward and she was being nice to him. He suddenly wished that he could tell her about Angela. His wife was the sort of person who ought to have a good job. Maureen had been on TV. His wife ought to have been on TV, with her voice. To hear her sing, it was like hearing the angels singing. No, that was a crap way of putting it. Maybe Maureen, with her journalistic background, would have a better way of

54

expressing it. He tried to imagine Maureen, microphone in hand, reporting live on Angela's singing, with respect and enthusiasm, and a neat turn of phrase.

He couldn't remember the last time Angela had sung anything. He would go home and ask her to sing.

'I'd like to come back here, Maureen.'

'Oh yes, of course.'

'It doesn't happen all at once. You don't sit here and say yes or no, tick a box. It has to be assessed properly. You know?'

'Of course.'

Maureen was very calm but he could detect the eagerness. She was sharp, she had worked out that there was a chance. He hadn't said no. She had realised that however many parts there were to the test, she and Christina were through to the next round.

'Right, then.'

'Could I ask you, then, sir...' That rankled with him now and embarrassed him, that 'sir'. She wasn't a subservient, ignorant woman who called him sir by default, as he had assumed when he came in. She was an intelligent, desperate woman who was trying to flatter him.

'You can call me Lucas.'

'Oh, right. Thank you.' She didn't dare, though. Good for her. He'd have hated her for it. 'Could you tell me, typically, how long? I mean, I'm not pressing you...'

'I don't know. Maybe a couple of months.'

'Oh, right.'

He didn't want to toy with her. He wanted to do something nice. 'The thing is – at the end... I mean, I can't say...'

'No. Of course not. Still, we'd rather live with hope. You see, I believe–'

'What has she got? I mean, is it a disease?'

Maureen's face. Honestly. He hadn't meant it like that. Her face twisted as if he'd just punched her in the guts.

'I'm sorry. It's just, we have to know. For the reports.' They didn't.

'No. She's... it was something in the womb. Or maybe at birth. You know how it is with the midwives now, the care.'

'What's the prognosis? Will she get any better?'

'I don't know.'

'She won't get worse, will she?'

'Well, it's not good, actually. Nobody thought she'd survive; that she'd be here this long.'

'Oh, poor little thing.'

'She doesn't suffer.'

'No. Good.'

He went over to the child and bent over her, all smiles. 'Goodbye, Christina,' he said. He led Maureen outside.

A sad thought had occurred to him. 'Maureen, I've got to say this.' Did he? Well, he'd started now. Besides, he liked the woman. 'If you're looking for me to help Christina... If you think maybe you can get connections, someone to help you, through me...'

She'd been looking anxious. Maybe she thought he was going to walk outside the door with her and say no, I'm not coming back after all, it's not a miracle. Now she smiled, her face one big Nike swoosh of a smile. She thought he was kind and sweet and she was delighted because he hadn't denied her disabled daughter her chance of being declared a miracle.

'No,' she said. 'No, Lucas, it's nothing like that. Thank you.'

So, they were on first name terms. And he was for some reason going to go back to that house again and prolong everyone's agony, including his own.

He got in the car and went home to Angela. Why didn't she sing any more and why hadn't she got pregnant? Those were two things that he wanted to know. He would ask her.

8

Spare Us the Granny

Darling,

The time has come. We must leave – now, before the borders close. Don't underestimate the danger. I think this is our last chance. You can bring the kid but we must leave now. I have friends in Adelaide who will look after us. The last boat leaves in two days' time. You know I've tried to persuade M to go? We could all go together but he's adamant that he won't leave. You try. But if he won't come, please come with me. I have the tickets.

Just so we're clear, I have tickets for three adults and one child. If you can't persuade M, I'll give his ticket away at the dock. Someone will be glad of it – although it's a horrible thought that my gift might split up a couple hoping to go away together, with one being left behind. No, let's be positive. Perhaps it means a family who already have tickets will be able to bring Granny with them, or some other spare relative. Best of all, M will be there with you and we'll all leave together.

You understand me, though? I have bought a ticket for M because I don't want there to be any reason for you not to come with me.

I love you.

J xx

p.s. You know I won't care if you continue to live with M in Australia. We can sort out the domestic arrangements when we get to the other side. I haven't bought tickets with a view to buying a place for you at my side. This is the last chance out of here, for all of us. Be there!

p.p.s. It'll be crowded on the docks. I'll wear flowers in my hair so you'll easily be able to spot me. I'll build a trembling, conical tower of brightly-coloured blossoms on my head, so that as I stalk through the crowd looking for you, fragrant petals will scatter in my wake. I hope to generate enough interest with my striking new look to be able to found a religion on board, to while away the hours on our passage to the promised land. Wear flowers in your hair or don't, my darling – I'll be able to find you by the warmth of your smile. But be there. Be there. I love you xxx

p.p.p.s. If you have trouble getting through security without tickets, tell them you're booked in cabin 2.012 under my name. I suppose it means that if I have to give away M's ticket, we'll have a granny travelling with us in our cabin? Please persuade him to come to spare us the granny. I can almost hear the song that he and I would compose together to celebrate being spared the granny. Another way to pass the time on the voyage while other less inventive people are playing Scrabble. See how good we'll be together, we three plus little El? We'll have a roaring good time.

One final note (too many pees, sorry) – we can still make a difference over there. We're not deserting the cause, just re-grouping. But we can't stay here. Remember: you can't make a difference when you're dead.

9 Jesmond

Jesmond was standing on a low stage in an underground venue where he'd been invited to give a reading of his poetry. He was rocking from side to side, like a mother trying to comfort her baby. He was wearing black jeans and a black jumper. He had the thumb of one hand hooked into the pocket of his jeans. The other hand held a glass of red wine, which sloshed about a bit but didn't spill, despite the gentle rocking, because his hand acted like a gimble, his elbow the hinge.

Jesmond unhooked his free hand and wiped it through his hair from the crown to the tip of his curls, then smiled, as if verifying the length and vigour of his wiry grey hair had reassured him in some way. He took a sip from the glass of wine, then put it down.

'Friends,' he said. 'Friends.'

People stopped talking and looked around. Strictly speaking, most of them weren't friends at all, but a collection of strangers who formed part of his audience. But as he was standing on stage, calling out to them, they had little choice but to look at him, and by doing so, it was as if they accepted that they *were* his friends. By such subtle little tricks, he managed to get his audience on side before he had even started.

He was there to read his poetry. But he didn't read it in a monotone from a piece of paper held in his hand, as some poets did. He performed it, from memory. Whether or not that was for practical reasons – no paper meant no evidence to be seized in case of a raid – it nevertheless meant he could make eye contact, he could give the appearance of speaking from the heart, could even seem to be making it up especially for those listening, there and then, on the spot. Jesmond had discovered that the best way to appear sincere was to be sincere. When he performed, he really, really meant it. And that's how he could cry, and make others cry, when he said the things he did.

So far as his poetry was concerned, it was a bit hit and miss. But that's poetry for you. People were rarely disappointed as they hadn't necessarily come to hear his poetry, they had come to participate in a minor act of rebellion. They had come to see a famous man give a fine performance of his work, just for them. He made no money from it. Some said he did it for idealistic reasons, some said he did it because he craved the attention. What people believed had little to do with Jesmond; it was a reflection of their general point of view.

Looking at him, hearing him call out at the beginning, 'Friends, friends,' you would think he would go on to command the room in an almost military style. He always refused to use a microphone. But he spoke very softly – another trick. His audience had to lean forward to listen.

They had to keep very still and silent to be sure to make out all the words. Even the rustle of an anorak was enough to distort what he was saying. There were no pause or rewind buttons on a live performance, as his young audience came to appreciate as they strained to listen to him. They had to pay attention if they wanted to follow what was being said.

Jesmond was beautiful the way an antique is beautiful, just by being old. The young people looked at him and thought, 'I wish he was my father.' Not because he was a poet and that was cool, but because their own fathers had disappeared, died or were in prison and he was about the right age to step in as a substitute.

The young people stood about in their jeans and jumpers and looked up at Jesmond. They were men, mostly, although the androgynous look was very popular these days and so you could never be sure. Later, when they discussed his performance and his appearance, more than one would remark that his head seemed to be square in shape. Jesmond had overheard it said so often, he'd begun to think his head must resemble a novelty watermelon grown by the Japanese, which it did not. He was an old man with a large jaw, big fleshy ears and grey hair, that was all. But the young people weren't used to seeing old men. Jesmond seemed as ancient and mysterious to them as the giant leatherback turtles Jesmond had seen on a beach in Malaysia in his youth. The turtles returned to the same beaches, year after year, to lay their eggs in the moonlight, remnants from the dinosaur age. Seeing those turtles' eyes wet with tears,

Jesmond had thought that the turtles were crying with emotion, just as the woman he'd loved said she had done when she gave birth. More practical observers attributed the tears to the practicalities of laying eggs on a beach, and the need to keep the sand out of the mother turtles' eyes.

As he read his poetry, tears were sliding down Jesmond's cheeks tonight. Many of the young people cried with him. If he had yawned a lot on stage, might they have yawned, also?

'Rise up,' Jesmond urged them as he reached the chorus of his most famous poem, published in a book entitled *This Faerie England*. 'Rise up and be free.' And when they heard him say it, in that dark basement that he had visited at some risk to his personal freedom, it seemed to most of the audience that it was the least they could do.

Unfortunately, there were some who interpreted the chorus as a 'Simon Says' moment of light entertainment. They tried to show their approval of the concept of rising up by actually rising up, getting to their feet or, if they were already standing, going up on the balls of their feet, lifting their hands and joining in with his words. The most defiant thing about it was the way they pointed their chins upwards. If Jesmond had asked them to shake their booty, they might have done that. There were some people, Jesmond was always left reflecting, who probably didn't deserve to be set free.

His eyes searched the audience. He craved the company of women at these things. It was difficult to tell who was who, of course. That skinny 'indie band' look was very popular, and Jesmond could understand why, but still he didn't like it; at any moment, one expected them to pick up a guitar and sing some nasal lament that referenced brand names – or, at least, one would if this were thirty years earlier. The other thing that was interesting was the craze for thinness. Everyone had worried so much that a trend towards obesity that had began about thirty years ago would continue and continue until everyone could only waddle. But each generation rebels against the last, and this one was no different. Besides, lives were at stake. Adding weight to a body was like a litmus test for gender. Fat went on different areas for women than it did for men. Fat betrayed those who wanted to keep that kind of information hidden so they could go out at night. So the young stayed slim. Young men grew their hair. Young women kept theirs short. Jeans and loose tops were popular, as were scarves around the throat, to disguise the Adam's apple. Not wearing a beard was an act of rebellion for the men, a way of showing solidarity with women.

Jesmond didn't have a beard but then no one would mistake him for a woman. He was a grizzled, old, ugly man. His teeth were yellow, like the keys on a disused piano in a church hall, the kind that would have been played during amateur dramatic rehearsals and ballet classes in the old days. The yellowing of Jesmond's teeth was attributable to his advancing age, his use of tobacco and red wine, not disuse. But perhaps the young people, with their shiny white teeth, connected the state of his teeth to cultural neglect. There were no more ballet classes, no little girls in pink leotards doing their jetés and pliés, and there were no more poets like Jesmond.

He was surprised to see someone he thought he recognised in the audience. An elderly lyricist who had once written for jazz musicians, a grande dame of the poetry scene. Or at least she had been, a quarter of a century ago. He hoped she wouldn't recognise him. She herself was not instantly recognisable. She was folded in on herself like an envelope, she had a deeply lined face and she was wearing a turban in kingfisher colours. Perhaps there was some performance art aspect to her outfit: she had come as a living painting? 'The Princess' they used to call her, or sometimes 'La Princesse' because she was European and rather imposing. He hoped she wouldn't stay to hear his set. She was the superior poet and she knew it. He couldn't have said he actually wanted the police to burst in and arrest her for being out after the curfew – for one thing, they'd probably have taken half the audience with them if they did. But an incident like that would solve his problems.

He seemed to remember kissing her once. Did they have sex? He couldn't remember. He only remembered a cherry liqueur taste to her mouth, while at the same time acknowledging it was absurd, an indulgence of old age to coat a memory with such a thing. He felt the saliva glands at the sides of his mouth prick at the memory – the false memory – of that cherry sweetness.

But she knew him. She could see him looking at her. She pushed her stick into the ground. A stick. Christ, how much time had passed since they'd seen each other? She stood up and walked over to him.

She had always treated him with condescension, as he remembered it. But now she was smiling graciously, tears in her eyes.

'How you people have suffered. You were always a great man, Jesmond. But to do this...'

A poetry reading? He searched her crepy old face for a hint that she was mocking him. Or perhaps she was merely insincere, like one of those annoying people who have been brought up to be polite, the sort who used to come round to his house for a spaghetti Bolognese in student days and gush on and on and on about how delicious it was and ask for the recipe. But she was sincere, moved. The tears sparkling in her eyes proclaimed it, and the coppery crème eyeshadow glittering in the folds of her eyelids complimented the tears very nicely, in a slightly gaudy way. Her whole eye area was like a muted indoor firework display. He could have plucked her eyeballs from the sockets and strung them up and set them twirling with the tears still on them and they could have served as disco balls for fairies or other tiny creatures in some miniature dance hall.

Her fingers were splayed sideways by arthritis, so when she held them up, it looked as if she was about to make a kooky, self-deprecating joke. He took hold of her hands to pull her towards him, and he kissed her and – extraordinary miracle – he got a faint taste of cherry on her lips, something artificially sweet and fiery. It must be some lozenge she habitually ate, and had been sourcing and sucking on for more than twenty-five years. Extraordinary. He ran his tongue along his lips. Unless it was lip gloss? Did women of her age wear lip gloss or had that fallen out of fashion, linked to a time of pop stars and triviality? She noticed him smiling. She nodded once, very slowly. What was she acknowledging, exactly? She might have thought the kiss reminded him of their earlier tryst. She looked relieved, touched, grateful, as if she had remained young in one man's heart. He couldn't ask about the cherry taste, it would have been unchivalrous. She would go home tonight and look in the mirror before she rubbed the cream on her face to take off her make-up, and she would think, 'You've still got it, girl.' Whatever else he was, he was enough of a gentleman to let her have her dreams. After all, she had restored his to him with one kiss. It seemed that his other sugar-coated – cherry-coated, if you will – memories might not be the foolish reminiscences of an old man. Maybe she (not The Princess but *she*) had loved him as much as he remembered she had.

He suddenly felt flustered, wished he had not entrusted the letters to Lucas's wife. What had he been thinking? He always used to swear that he would not part with them until he died. It was only recently that he had come to see it as absurd that he was hoarding letters from *himself*. But he had come to a decision – he shivered, felt almost a superstition about it – he would return to Lucas's the following day and ask to have the journal back. Lucas wouldn't have read them, anyway (at any rate, he hoped not, because if so, he might have guessed the identity of the woman Jesmond had been writing to) so he might as well keep them with him. The memories would die with him, when the time came.

10 The Pie

Angela looked so lovely when Lucas got home. She'd been baking something. She had flour on her nose. The wife in his imagination and the woman he was married to were never quite the same person. Maybe it was OK to fantasise about other women because even when you fantasised about your own wife, you weren't really fantasising about her, you were fantasising about a fantasy.

She seemed cheerful today, not so beaten down as she'd seemed in recent weeks. He was cheerful, too. She noticed it.

'Your miracle people not so annoying as usual?'

'I met this woman; she used to read the news on TV.'

'You're kidding? How old is she?'

'She's not so old. I reckon she'd have been quite young back then. She was just starting out, she said.'

'What's she do now, then?'

'She takes care of her kid. This disabled kid.'

Angela looked sad at that. Shit. So now he couldn't ask her about getting pregnant because she'd be thinking of the kid.

Look, nobody was saying they didn't want a disabled kid. Nobody was saying that. It's just you didn't want your kid to have anything less than another person's kid, and that included speech and mobility and all the rest of it. The thing was, with antenatal care the way it was in London – i.e. non-existent – infant mortality and death in childbirth and previously avoidable complications leading to disability in the child, they were all a very real possibility. People started to question whether it was a good idea to bring a child into the world. First, because it might be a short journey with a sad ending. Second, because if the kid did make it past their first year, they might not have a very happy life, especially if they were a girl.

'Did you mean it, what you said?' he asked her. 'About doing something about it if you were pregnant and you had a girl?' Some people smothered the kid at birth if it was a girl. It was frowned on but people did it.

'I never said that.' She was shocked.

'No, but you said something about having a girl – not wanting one.'

'Did I? You must have misunderstood.'

He was having the conversation he hadn't wanted to have. 'Let's not talk about it. What's for tea? I'm hungry.'

'I'm making a pie.'

'Ooh, lovely.'

She wasn't an idiot, though. She wouldn't leave it. 'I didn't say I'd kill our child if it was a girl.'

'No.'

'What made you say it, then?'

'There was this girl today, she was disabled.'

'You think I'd kill a child because it was disabled?' She screeched the words. She was incredulous.

'No, I'm not saying that.'

'What then?'

'No, there was this girl – this lovely disabled girl – and I thought "I wish we could have a child," and I wondered why we haven't.' It took him by surprise. He was nearly crying. He had to turn away so she wouldn't see. He pretended to do the washing up. He put some water in the sink. He wished he hadn't thought all those horrible things about dunking Maureen's head in a sink full of washing up, and the baked beans. He had no reason to think she even fed baked beans to her family. It was snobbish of him. It's because he'd thought she was poor and ignorant, before he realised she used to read the news on TV. He wondered if people thought that Angela was stupid because she didn't have a job to give her any status. They wouldn't think it if they'd ever heard her sing.

'And you don't ever sing any more.' He actually was crying. She came and put her arms around him, put her head against his back between his shoulder blades. There was no use pretending he wasn't upset. He had his hands in the soapy water in the sink but there was no use pretending. At least now she knew he was crying, he wouldn't have to do the washing up.

He dried his hands on a tea towel. They went and sat down at the kitchen table. He could smell the pie in the oven. A fish pie with a mashed potato topping. She had made it just for him. He was a lucky man and yet he was crying over this disabled child or because he couldn't have one of his own, disabled or not. Or because it had been such a long time since he had heard Angela sing.

'We have to get out of here,' she said.

'I know.'

'No, you don't know. Something happened.'

'What do you mean?'

'A man came here today. He said he knew you.'

'Who?'

'He said his name was Jones. Lucas, are you alright? Do you know him?'

'What did he say?'

'He had a knobbly face. An ugly man, quite friendly. Lucas?'

'What did he say?'

'Just that he knew you. Well, it was quite strange, really.'

'What did he want? Did you let him in the house?'

'No, of course I didn't.'

He was up on his feet now, preparing himself for what she might say. He was so angry and frightened and murderous – that fiend, Jones, here with his wife – that his head was buzzing. A million wasps with chainsaws, inside his head. His fists were clenched. His face was red, that rosy flush on the skin that he had so wished to see on Jones's wife. Spit had collected at the corners of his mouth. His breathing was altered.

'Lucas, what is it?'

'What did he do to you?'

'Nothing.'

'What did he say?'

'Lucas, sit down. You're going mad. What's the matter? He just came by, he said he knew you. Said they were looking in on all the wives, just checking to see if they were OK.'

'And did he... did he make any lewd suggestions to you?'

She stifled a giggle. She could see that he was angry. But what he was saying was funny to her.

'Did he try to touch you? Angela? It's important.'

'I'm not a child, Lucas.'

'Would you tell me?'

'Lucas, what's the matter with you? He came to see if I was OK. He said they were worried about the security of the wives. He told me to call him if I couldn't get hold of you while you were away.'

'He gave you his phone number?'

'He gave me his business card.'

'Let me see.'

She went to the kitchen drawer, the one with the napkins and the tea towels. They kept a few take-away menus, flyers from people offering their services as gardeners, decorators, handymen. You needed them these days as it was so difficult for women to go out and shop, even for food. There was no question of a woman going to a hardware store; she might as well hang a red light over the door for all the opprobrium she'd be likely to suffer in the community.

Angela looked in the drawer for a few moments, moved the things around in there. Was she just pretending it wasn't readily to hand? She took out the business card. She handed it over.

Jonathan Jones, it said. Head of Security.

'Did he talk about his wife?'

'Well, no. He said he was worried about her. That's all.'

'Did he tell you her name?'

'He said, "We're worried about the wives. I'm a married man myself." That kind of thing.'

'I'm sorry.'

'Why are you so angry? What's he done?'

'No, you don't understand.'

'Well tell me, then.'

'He films his wife and broadcasts it in the office.'

'Oh God.'

'I've seen her soaping her tits in the shower, Angela. I've seen the hairs on her–'

'Don't be… Honestly, Lucas. Don't.'

'What, don't say cunt?'

'No. There's no need.'

'He's a cunt. I've seen his wife's cunt. I don't want him looking at yours.'

He stormed upstairs. So that she wouldn't see him in such a state, as much as anything else.

'Lucas?' she called up after him, the flour on her nose, the pie in the oven – the perfect wife.

He shouted down the stairs at her: 'Cunt.'

So that was that, then – no singing from Angela that night.

He went to bed without bathing, getting under the covers and switching off the light even though it was far too early to sleep. There was something else that was annoying him, something just outside his normal perception, that he only ever thought about just as he was about to fall off to sleep… That was it! He turned on the light and reached under the bed. A fat leather-bound journal full of dangerous, seditious ideas that would get them both put away forever if someone like Jones ever got in here and saw them. He pulled all the pages out of the binding. He took them and the letters and stormed downstairs.

Angela was surprised to see him in his pyjamas with the papers Jesmond had left for him. She knew what they were as soon as she looked at him, although she misunderstood his motivation for destroying them. 'Lucas,' she said. 'Please.'

Lucas went to the bookcase and took his only copy of Jesmond's famous book, *This Faerie England* – inscribed to him by the great man himself – from its hiding place behind the copies of the Children's Encyclopaedia vols five to seven that Angela set so much store by.

He got a torch from a drawer in the kitchen, and some fire lighters from where they lay on top of the coal in the copper bucket next to the fireplace in the front room. He went into the back garden and lit a bonfire in the brazier. He put some twigs and leaves on the flames and then tossed Jesmond's notes, letters and book into it.

Random words caught his eye as the pages fell: faerie, spoiled, darling, Matthew.

When most of the pages had burned, he went inside, wiped his slippers on the mat, double-locked the door to the garden. One danger, at least, had been averted.

11 Why

Now that Lucas had destroyed the letters, Angela wasn't going to go crazy wondering what had happened. Jesmond was still here in London, after all; it seemed pretty obvious that he hadn't made it to Adelaide with his girlfriend and her child. The *what* wasn't important. Angela was interested in *why*. She was surrounded by millions of people in London and she never got a chance to enquire into why they did the things they did. They hid their true face from her. She could draw her own conclusions but she never really knew. She'd thought she might have a chance to know someone really well by reading Jesmond's letters. She had been looking forward to going on the journey with him.

It was only a story, for her. For Jesmond, it was his life. She wondered whether he had ever found out why his girlfriend never turned up at Southampton to get on the boat with him. Perhaps she was detained. Perhaps she couldn't bear to leave her husband. Perhaps she had underestimated the dangers facing them and the rest of the country and hadn't taken his letter seriously. Perhaps she had turned up and Jesmond had got cold feet and he wasn't there. Perhaps they were intercepted on their way to the docks and made to turn back, either by her husband or by police road blocks. Perhaps the boat never sailed and they had to go back to their own lives and pretend the chance had never been offered to them.

She found it perplexing that Lucas wasn't more interested in Jesmond's welfare. With older people in such short supply in London, parents and godparents, even the parents of friends were usually treated with reverence. Lucas seemed to have no sympathy for the man at all. Didn't he wonder why things had turned out the way they had for him?

And then she thought, perhaps Lucas wasn't curious because he *knew* why. There was some secret, some family secret about his mother and his father and his godfather that he hadn't told her. Very well, she would get to the bottom of it.

12 Drinking

When Jesmond finished his set, there was always a moment of intense loneliness. He bent and picked up his glass, drained it. A young chap stepped up at the end, diffident. Despite the apparent diffidence, Jesmond was nervous as he came near. You never knew who these people were and what dangers they might represent. Jesmond felt chilly, like a man induced by a nuisance caller to step out of the bath and stand at the front door in his dressing gown. He wished the lad would go away but almost as soon as he wished it, more of them came up, as if he had wished on a faulty talisman and triggered the opposite of what he wanted.

'Fancy a drink, then?' one of the lads asked him.

Jesmond always wanted a drink after a gig. Drinking provided a wonderfully immersive experience, drugs too, although they were harder to get hold of. Few other things took you over like that. Sex, yes. But certain factors needed to be in place to make that happen, namely, a more-than-passing interest in the now-fatiguing act of love on his part and the consensual involvement of other(s). Drinking, though sociable, was something that could be experienced alone. And it was democratising; the tipsy delights of the first drink available to anyone for the price of a glass of wine or a whisky. But tonight he would not drink alone.

Jesmond felt obliged to play up to the flamboyance that might be expected of a man of his status and colourful reputation. He stood on the edge of the stage and said, 'Young man, I thoroughly approve of drinking because drinking leads to drunkenness, and that causes one to make mistakes. Mistakes bring wisdom, or learning from them does. So, let's drink.'

The kids loved it. Jesmond didn't necessarily believe any of it any more, although perhaps he once had. Loss made you wiser and sadder. And he had experienced so much of it. Perhaps he should say something about that? But they were grinning at him, happy enough with his pronouncements. He wanted to say something about how things weren't quite so inherently funny once you got to his age. Drink made him repeat himself, so there was no need to say everything all at once, he could save some of it for later on in the evening, when the subject would inevitably come round again.

They took him to a room at the back and poured some rather cheap wine into a plastic cup and gave it to him. Too late, he remembered he had left his glass on the stage, from where it had no doubt been cleared by now and stacked into the dishwashing machine. Drinking wine from a plastic cup was as dissatisfying as kissing a woman wearing an orthodontic brace but there was nothing he could do about it now. At least it wasn't Styrofoam.

There were a few young men already in the back room, two with acoustic guitars. Candles flickered on the tables. It was like a bohemian fantasy. He felt intensely happy for a few moments.

'Jesmond?' someone said, a very eager look on his face.

'Uh, gimme a moment,' Jesmond said. 'Takes a while to wind down after a gig. Imagine a jagged line on a graph in a recession.'

The kids stared at him. One of them handed him a joint. He smoked it. He drank from the plastic cup. He used his thumb and forefinger to wipe at the granular deposits that collected at the sides of his mouth. He felt the red wine flood the veins in his face, like those light-up street maps of London that had been popular with tourists, before the sight of a tourist in London became an anomaly. The joints in his fingers ached, particularly the top knuckle of the little finger on his right hand, and the thumb knuckle on his left hand. Still, he felt happy. Was this happiness his reward? He couldn't say why he did it, otherwise. Once he would have said he did it to inspire others.

He looked up. He had recovered and was ready to engage with them.

'What you writing, Jesmond?' They wanted to admire him. But he hadn't written anything in months. No – years. He smiled and looked bashful, batting at the air in front of his face as if to dispel a thick layer of lies that hung about in front of his face, to prevent himself spreading them around as he breathed, spoiling a potentially pleasant evening.

The two boys with guitars began to sing. Jesmond was on safer ground, here. People only ever wanted to hear the old protest songs that he'd written with Matthew, all those years ago. They never asked if he was working on another one of those. Like fans at a music gig, they didn't want new songs; they wanted the old stuff, the familiar stuff they could join in with.

Like the poetry, the protest songs enjoined listeners to rise up. Pretty much the only difference between the poetry and the protest songs was that the songs had a melody attached. Well, otherwise they wouldn't have been songs, would they?

Everyone in the back room drank too much wine. Most sang. At events like these, people sometimes made the mistake of telling Jesmond how much they loved the tunes of the protest songs, thinking that they would endear themselves to him. People were so silly sometimes. He had written the lyrics, Matthew had set them to music. Admiring the music in Jesmond's songs was like going to a barbecue at a man's house and admiring the design of the garden next door. It was not pertinent and it was most definitely not a way to win favour.

But these kids were OK. They didn't praise the music specifically. They let him know how much they loved the songs by the way they sang them. They belted out the stirring bits. They closed their eyes when they sang the moving bits. They punched the air or held hands, as appropriate. When they got to the chorus of the most famous one (entitled, fittingly enough, *Rise Up*) the musicians showed their reverence for the words by stopping their strumming and beating out the rhythm with the palms of their open hands on their guitars as they sang a capella. They sang with conviction. Jesmond had noticed that when men spent the evening singing rousing songs with other men, it tended to make them feel that victory was possible. In the early days he'd believed it was a good sign and that it meant these men would join the cause. But it hadn't happened. They'd just gone home again, as if singing was an end in itself. Maybe they remembered a time when you could still go to football matches, and the crowd would sing to urge their teams to victory, and take some of the credit for it when they did, and boo them when they lost. But singing was no way to seal victory in a revolution and it was certainly no substitute for action.

Imagine a land for you and meee, sang the assembled group.

Without borders or checks on our ID

Imagine no CCTeeVeee.

Jesmond felt dirty and sweaty and tired. He was neither wealthy nor healthy. He was an old man, on the run. What was it all for? Was it really for these moments when – if not actually happy – at least everyone seemed to believe in the possibility of happiness?

The possibility of happiness. The phrase made him think of the woman he had once loved very much. Jesmond felt choked. It would almost be easier if someone were to come in and kill him now, or arrest him and take him away. He wouldn't have to carry on. He wouldn't have to bother with the burden of it. But then he thought, maybe he really had been wishing on a faulty talisman all these years because there never was any intervention to force him to give up his life, and so he endured. Still, he didn't want to die. Not really, not while there was a chance that the woman he had loved was still alive. Deep in his heart, he still hoped for a reconciliation. Was that why he called for reunification of this country? Because he thought it might lead to a more personal kind of 'reunification'?

Sometimes he thought he was a fraud. Hiding it from other people was tiring but it seemed better than announcing it and making those who admired him miserable as well. He wasn't lying, he was trying not to disappoint.

There was a lull in the music while a lad changed a string on his guitar. Someone came up to him.

'Jason Prince,' the lad said, putting out his hand. Presumably that was the lad's name – it wasn't Jesmond's.

'Hi, Jason,' he said.

'Good crowd tonight. Packed, wasn't it? I'm sorry the place is so small. Security, y'know?'

'I know.'

'What's more important, would you say, reaching a wide audience or reaching an audience who really gets what you're saying?'

'Son, I want as many people as possible to hear what I have to say. It's not relationships I'm after, it's an audience. You piss about worrying who's here and whether they're worthy of hearing it, you're gonna lose it.'

'You get a buzz, doing this?'

'Not really. It gets to be more like a duty. Like being a preacher, not a pop star. You know?'

The boy looked disappointed.

'Maybe it's a buzz at the beginning,' Jesmond conceded.

'I write poetry.'

Oh great. Jesmond looked around for a means to escape the inevitable.

'I can't deliver it like you can. I can't do it justice. I know it's an imposition but could you spare an hour or two, to teach me? I mean, I'm not saying it only takes a couple of hours. But if you could give up the time.'

'Uh, probably not. Practice is all. Get up there and do it. You'll find your way.'

Jason offered his poem for Jesmond to read. He took it from an embroidered pouch that hung from a leather thong around his neck, under his T-shirt, and when he passed it to Jesmond, it was warm to the touch.

Jason Prince said, 'I wish I could learn from you.'

'I travel alone,' said Jesmond, somewhat pompously, even to his own ears. 'If you want to learn from me, you have to be able to find me. If you can find me, so can they.' But a man gets to be a certain age, he wants to have a son. If he can't have a son, he'll have a substitute, and acquiring an acolyte was likely to be a much more expeditious method than any other. He would be the boy's mentor. His master. He felt a fizzy, excited feeling just thinking about it, like a dose of baking soda going through his veins.

Jesmond read the poem. It wasn't what he was expecting at all.

The paper it was written on had a scent of the boy's body, animal but not repugnant, like a much-loved pet moments after it has got up from sleep to rub itself against your leg. Jesmond touched that paper and then he read the poem and he felt it was the start of something. He had been called to witness a momentous event whose humble signifier was these handwritten words on a warm page.

Jesmond's verse was rousing, like rugby songs, except with a social message. But when he read the words Jason Prince had written, he felt the breath and blood being slowly squeezed out of him, as if a giant rubber sheath was being rolled over him, over his head, over arms clamped tightly to his sides.

'You OK, man?' asked Jason, anxious.

Jesmond looked up at him, mouth downturned, eyes shimmering with tears. He put one fat finger up to the lower lid of his left eye and a tear rolled out of it and down his face, followed by others, dampening his finger and the cheek his finger rested on. The thing about Jesmond was that he should have been an actor, rather than a poet. Perhaps he only wrote so that he'd have a chance to perform his work.

'Young man,' said Jesmond, 'there's nothing I can teach you. Reading your poem is like picking up a snow globe only to see that there's a real city encased in that delicate structure, behind the glass. This is beautiful. You have an extraordinary talent. You have nothing left to learn.'

Jason's face transformed, unexpectedly and swiftly, like a Japanese paper flower that blossoms and 'grows' when dropped into water. He leant forward and gripped Jesmond's arm above the bicep. He nuzzled his face into the shoulder seam of Jesmond's jumper. He seemed to be totally overcome. He gripped too hard and nuzzled too long. Jesmond wondered if this was a gay thing. Fame had a strange effect on people, and he was famous, after all. Perhaps Jason had not written those lines but had copied them out of a book to impress him. It might have been Keats or Yeats or Shelley, one of those. An obscure poem from a master. If only you could still get access to the internet, you used to be able to check things like that in an instant.

Jason lifted his head at last, so he could speak. The side of his face was a bit crumpled and red, as if his cheek had been patched with corduroy. His ear was also red. 'When I wrote it, I was thinking of you,' said Jason, as if he could hear Jesmond's thoughts and wanted to reassure him. 'I was inspired by you.'

If he was going to claim the verse as his, that was alright. That made it his responsibility; it wasn't up to Jesmond to check whether it was actually true. Jesmond rather looked forward to being the innocent in all this, if it turned out Jason wasn't the author of the verse. He was sick and tired of feeling the fraud, of being older and more cynical than everyone else. He almost hoped that

Jason was duping him. It would restore him to innocence, if so. And if not, then those beautiful, beautiful words would uplift him. He'd make the boy his friend, his apprentice. They'd travel the length and breadth of London, break into the parks and sit by the lakes. The boy would read him his poetry. He would die a happy man.

'What's your name?' The boy had told him but he couldn't be expected to remember the name of every would-be poet who came up to him after a gig.

'It's Prince. Jason Prince.'

'That's apposite. A new ruler. A new star in town.' Jesmond was a bit drunk. He had swigged and refilled that plastic cup several times. He had drunk from it steadily, grimly, as if it was his duty to get rid of the cheap wine so it couldn't hurt any of them any more. The part of his brain that believed that he was 'helping' in some way, by drinking as much of the stuff as he could, never seemed to learn that there was always another bottle to be uncorked (or unscrewed).

'How will I find you?' Jason asked.

'I move around a lot.'

'I could leave a message for you at a safe house. Or a public place; a pub or a restaurant or something.'

Jesmond was amused. 'I'll give you an address. Have you got something to write on?'

The boy offered his page of poetry.

'I can't,' said Jesmond, simply. The words were too beautiful. He wasn't going to write over the top of them.

'There's a little space on the end. Write on that.'

Jesmond wrote an address, very small, at the end of the piece of paper, and handed it back. 'You can ask here. They might know where I am.'

The boy stared at the address, put the paper back into the fabric pouch around his neck. He saw Jesmond looking at him with longing and intensity. He took the paper, looked at the address on the bottom for a few moments, committing it to memory, then handed the page back to Jesmond. 'You can keep it,' he said. 'If you like.'

The paper felt silky and warm. Jesmond would have liked to put it next to his heart but he was wearing a jumper without a pocket, no shirt underneath. The only method he could think of, therefore, that would keep the page close to his heart would be to tuck the paper under his armpit; impractical for so many reasons. He put it into his trouser pocket, the one where he liked to hook his thumb when his hand was idle when he was doing a reading. He didn't know what the boy made of him plunging the paper penis-wards into his pocket and keeping it there, next to his groin. Perhaps he didn't make anything of it, although poets tended to concern themselves with imagery more than most. Jesmond shrugged – even when carrying out conversations with himself inside his head, he tended to embellish them with physical gestures, which made him appear more eccentric than perhaps he was.

'Can you help me get published, Jesmond?'

'That's what you want?'

'Yeah. You know, I can't believe this. It's a miracle I found you.'

It was indeed. Perhaps he could get the boy registered with Lucas. Hadn't the poets believed, in the old days, that the words of God were flowing through them? If he could get the boy acknowledged, he could get him protected. The arts would flourish. Theatre. Poetry. He would give readings, introduce the boy. They would print and distribute the books produced as a result of their creative partnership.

He stood, too quickly. He felt dizzy. He ran his hand from the crown of his head to the tip of his curls. He squeezed on the curls a few times, his fist gentle and rhythmic, like a milkmaid squeezing a teat. Perhaps he was testing for crispness. If so, he must have been disappointed. The curls were limp. He was drunk. He had to go home.

The young men in the club, seeing Jesmond on his feet, reverted to another chorus of 'Rise up, Rise up.' The words seemed almost mocking after what he had just read. Jesmond hiccupped and a small amount of peppery vomit rose up (ha ha) into his throat and went back down again. His view of the world had shrunk to a tiny letter-box shape directly in front of his eyes. He waved his hand and joined in with the song, while looking around for the door.

'You will remember my name?'

'I will.'

'I hope I can find you.'

'You found me tonight, lad.'

'I'd been looking for you for more than a year. Waiting to meet you.'

'That address I gave you should do it. Ask there, or leave a message.'

'It's not your home? Can't you tell me where you live?'

'I don't have a home. I move around.'

'How about, we choose a tree. I'll carve a message on a tree trunk and you'll find me.'

'It's actually quite hard work carving a message on a tree. Ever tried it?'

'But that way we could leave messages for each other without arousing suspicion.'

'Come with me.'

Now the boy was wondering.

'We can travel together. If you're with me, you'll know where to find me. Won't you?'

The boy didn't answer. He was thinking it over but he didn't look keen.

Jesmond put on his black leather jacket and turned to go. That baking soda fizzing in his veins again. That peppery magma. Limp curls. Letterbox vision. Why should the boy follow him? What was there to entice him? He'd said himself there was nothing he could teach him.

As he left, as he opened the door and closed it again behind him, he realised that in actual fact, he had been expecting the boy to come running after him, like a carpet salesman provoked by a customer determined to drive a hard bargain by leaving the shop. He realised that he hadn't really meant to leave. He had wanted the boy to come with him. And he realised that the boy wasn't coming because Jesmond had got the bargaining positions of their roles wrong. He was the carpet salesman, the one who wanted something. And in that case, he shouldn't have been the one to leave the shop. He wanted a happy ending, a fairytale, the boy – the Prince – running after him in the rain. Audrey Hepburn in *Breakfast at Tiffany's*.

'You are a fuck-up and a failure,' he said to himself, ashamed. He may have said the words in his head or he may have said them aloud. No matter, they were very nearly the last words he heard. A heavy instrument, a cricket bat or something like that, was brought down on the back of his head very hard. More blows on his arms and his shoulders. Thwack. Thwack, thwack. The sound of willow hitting leather (even if it was only Jesmond's old leather jacket) was redolent of a quaint old England that had long since disappeared, so it was quite a fitting sound to be coming from the author of *This Faerie England*, as if Jesmond had finally found his perfect moment as a performer; a human instrument, which when played would summon up reminders of the lost England he lamented in his poetry. Leather boots connected with the yellowing piano keys of his teeth, but this was less successful, instrumentally speaking. There was no melodic tinkle, no thundering crescendo of keys and chords. But then it takes a very skilled artist to play the piano with his boots, and Jesmond's attackers were thugs. Although it was impossible to say for sure, just by looking at them, whether or not any of the attackers could play an instrument, it was reasonable to assume that they could not, and furthermore, it was reasonable to assume that if they had attended more dutifully to music lessons as children, they might have had something more interesting to do to fill their time than beating up an old gentleman. But most of the schools in the state education system had closed down for fear of paedophiles. Music lessons likewise. These thugs were perhaps a product of their time.

Jesmond suddenly thought of something he would like to say. It seemed important. He was like a man who has been called to the stage at an awards ceremony and surprises himself by ripping up his speech and speaking from the heart. 'Life is a journey. A man may climb a mountain but what will he do when he gets to the top, except talk about how he got there?'

Then he thought of another way of putting it: 'Life is just a series of anecdotes.' Was that what he believed? What about love? Ordinarily he would have gestured to himself; a little shrug, a tilt of the head. But he wasn't in a position to do it as he was lying face down and someone – an unmusical thug – was standing on his right shoulder. Nor was he in any fit state to share his thoughts, unfortunately. His mouth was full of blood but anyway his brain was in such a mess, he probably couldn't have got a message to his tongue, even if he'd tried.

The narrow letterbox of his vision contracted until it was a tiny dot of light, then it went out, like an old-fashioned cathode ray television taking its time to settle down after it has been switched off.

Someone said the words, 'You fucking fascist.' He didn't hear them, which was probably a good thing. The last words he heard were his own, formulated inside his poor old, kicked-about, broken head but never spoken aloud: 'What about love?'

13   Ribena

The next day Lucas went into Jones's office, wondering if there would be any repercussions after his visit to Joanna. Jenkins was in there and both were drinking Ribena. It was supposed to be a super-drink; scientists had discovered that blackcurrants could help you live longer and make you more virile. Since most men died or disappeared before they were fifty years old, presumably it was the prospect of enhanced virility rather than longevity that interested everyone who had started drinking it, unless they believed they could somehow stop the soldiers at their door by pouring a line of blackcurrant syrup across the threshold.

Jones didn't behave like a man whose wife has been insulted. He offered Lucas a glass of the stuff and Lucas accepted. Well, why not? He liked the taste. He needed a little energy boost from all that sugar.

He couldn't see Jones's computer screen. Actually, to be fair, Jones didn't quite broadcast pictures of his wife. That's the way it had seemed, when Lucas had first got an eyeful of nipple. But, in fact, you had to go and stand at the other side of Jones's desk, and accidentally knock the keyboard to activate the screen, and then you had to know where to look among the icons on the screen; it was the one labelled JJ.

Jenkins was complaining about his job. It was what you had to do. You couldn't say you enjoyed what you did – that would have seemed like showing off – though you could mock other men's jobs so that listeners would infer that yours was better. Today Jenkins was doing this by expressing relief that he wasn't in charge of one of the vast and sprawling departments tasked with unravelling the familial ties claimed by London's women.

'See, my wife,' said Jenkins, 'she's Chinese.'

'Is she?' said Lucas.

Jenkins was one of those boorish people who believed that he was cleverer than everyone else just because he was too stupid to know how thick he was, so there was probably some trick involved here. Still, why not play along? Lucas was more than a match for him.

'Well, she spends all her time round the house of a Chinese woman she says is her sister. Ethnically, that makes her Chinese. See? She's Irish-looking as a bloody peat bog but she swears blind they're related. I wouldn't like to be in charge of it. Your wife, now...'

'She's black.'

Jenkins laughed uproariously, thinking they were sharing a riff on this joke about spurious ethnicity. Then he tailed off, unsure. He gave Lucas a funny look and then looked away. It was the reason some people didn't like Lucas and why they were also afraid of him, because they looked in his face and they could see he didn't give a shit about them. And then there was the job he did. The Miracle Inspector. No one was quite sure what that meant. Was it very important or one of those nonsensical jobs? Jenkins, for example, was in charge of something to do with cats that was enshrined in the constitution. People had the right to keep cats and Jenkins's job was to keep on top of it and make sure there were enough to go round and not too many, and so on. Rumour had it Jenkins spent most of his time rounding up spare cats and taking them off somewhere to be killed. He'd jump at the chance to be in a job that involved visiting women in their homes to discuss their prodigiously talented daughters and their 'special' sons, or to look at faces in their flans, of course he would.

'You seen the news?' asked Jones. The news was so heavily censored that almost no one saw it except Jones, which was why he liked to mention it. 'That poet's been killed. Anti-fascists, they think. Nihilists.'

Lucas paused for only a moment before pressing on: 'About the wives.'

'You knew him, didn't you?' said Jones to Lucas.

'Who?'

'Jesmond.'

'Jesmond's been killed?' Jenkins was incredulous. 'Shit. Man. You know what, I didn't even know he was still alive.'

'Yeah, exactly,' said Lucas. He was furiously angry. He hated everyone. Right there, right then, all he wanted to do was sit down in a chair and think quietly about Jesmond, his dad, his mum. What the man had meant to his family and what it meant that he was dead. But you had to keep up appearances. He stared back at Jones, evenly.

'Killed, though? Not detained?' This was Jenkins still bleating on about it, innocent as a little lamb.

'Kicked to death. Or beaten with a baseball bat. Or a bit of both,' Jones explained.

'They're sure it was him?' Lucas asked.

'Yeah. He was still recognisable.'

'Will there be a funeral?' asked Jenkins.

'I doubt it,' said Jones. 'They won't want a focus for insurgency. Clashes between the unionists and the nihilists. Load a singing in the streets. Crap like that.'

'No. Course not,' Jenkins agreed. 'Sad day, though? Man of his stature going like that. Say what you like about him. He had a rare talent.'

'Yes,' said Lucas bitterly. 'A talent for making alcohol disappear.' He felt angry, reckless. 'The wives,' he said. 'I've been thinking about their safety. It was something you said, Jones.'

Just because he was upset, there was no need to provoke Jones. He needed to calm down and be very careful about what he said.

'Are they in danger?' Jenkins was worried. Obviously no one had been round to his house recently to check out his salt of the earth Irish wife. Jenkins probably tried to make her feel like a princess by letting her keep two cats. Hopefully that was compensation for the fact that apparently no one wanted to see her naked.

'Got to keep an eye on them,' said Jones.

'You got surveillance equipment installed, Jenkins?' said Lucas.

'No. Have you?'

'No. Jones could help with that, though, couldn't you?'

'I could set something up for you.'

I bet you could, thought Lucas.

'If you let me know where to get the equipment,' said Jenkins, 'I'll sort it out.'

'He's got cameras,' Lucas said, of Jones.

Jenkins wasn't following this. He obviously hadn't seen Joanna's nipples. He was frowning and looking at Jones. 'You wouldn't put cameras on your wife, though?'

'See, I come from a security background,' Jones said. 'Say you go to a wedding in a hotel and the man sitting next to you, he's a fireman. Ask him where's the fire exits and he'll know. He'll come in your house and he'll be looking round – smoke alarm, exits.'

Jenkins didn't get it.

'Jones is a security man,' Lucas explained. 'An expert. He thinks about surveillance the way a fireman thinks about fire exits. You probably know an awful lot about cats.'

Jones was enjoying the idea of himself as an expert in something, and he chuckled at Lucas's put-down of Jenkins about the cats. He went to the drawer in his office. He got out a box of equipment and handed over two tiny cameras to Lucas, together with an equally tiny recording and transmitting device. 'Instructions in the box,' he said.

A thought occurred to Lucas as he took them. What if these cameras somehow transmitted to Jones as well as himself? 'They're secure? I mean, someone else couldn't hack in?'

'Best on the market. Totally secure.'

'Thanks, I'll... How much do I owe you?'

'No, no. Take it. Have it.'

So now he was in Jones's debt for camera equipment he had no intention of using. None whatsoever. Absolutely none. He looked at Jenkins. Perhaps Jenkins would try to keep up with the largesse by offering him a cat? But Jenkins was looking disappointed at not being offered free equipment to spy on his wife.

Jones's phone rang. Jones put on a 'top secret' face, so Lucas and Jenkins left the office together.

'Tell you what, Jenkins. Do you want it?'

'Really?'

'You have it, if you want. Didn't want to turn down old Jones in there. You know? But I don't need it.'

'You got something already?'

'Yeah, exactly. You have it. Don't want — sorry, what's her name, your missus?'

'Delilah.'

'Oh, really?'

'After that song. You know.'

'Well, you don't want her at home, worrying.'

'She can take care of herself, to be honest. Clap an intruder round the head with a frying pan.'

'It's not just the intruders. Some of the guys... some of them like to put the cameras in the bedroom.'

Jenkins bridled. He seemed to feel that Delilah's honour was at stake. 'Now hold on,' he said. 'Home porno?'

'Not just for the home, either. Some of the guys show it around.'

Jenkins goggled. Lucas watched the thoughts go round in Jenkins head like little fishes: The other 'guys', whoever that meant, were making home porno films of themselves with their wives and showing it round, though not to him? There he was, drinking Ribena in Jones's office and thinking he was in with the in crowd, and all the time there was some dirty little sex show going on that he wasn't invited to.

Would Jenkins now go home and record himself tupping his practical, sensible wife, and then try to show it to Jones as a way of getting further inside the inner circle in the Ministry? Lucas hoped so. He hoped he might get to see a bit of footage of Jenkins's wife naked, perhaps reclining on the bed, knickers off, legs open, frying pan in hand.

'They get quite competitive.'

'Do they? What is it, the wife in a nice pair of knickers, touching herself?'

'I think they, you know. They let the wives go round to each other's houses.'

'Oh, I see.'

'Does Delilah know Joanna?'

'Joanna? Is that your…?'

'Jones's wife. Lovely tits. Very lonely. Maybe your wife could…?'

102

'Oh, I see. Joanna. Where's she live, though?'

Oh God. What if this was a trap? Much as he would like Jenkins to send his wife round to Jones's to make saucy videos, maybe he shouldn't confess that he knew where Joanna lived.

'Arrange it through Jones.'

'How do you go about that, then?'

'Say your missus is lonely, can she go round to his wife. Don't say why. You see – and make sure Delilah knows this – they don't like it if it seems a set up. They're a load of Peeping Toms, they don't like to think it's a show. They can go to Piccadilly Circus for that. It's the innocence they like. The women, pure and innocent, soaping each other down in the shower.'

'Oh, I see.'

'And then it makes them feel kindlier to the parties involved. Like, if you ever wanted to get away from cats. I'm not saying. But if you did. You see? They'd remember you.'

'But your missus? Wouldn't it be easier if Delilah came round to yours, if she knows the ropes?'

He didn't want Jenkins's donkey wife – who might after all be a very nice person, but still – ordered round to his house and reluctantly trying to feel up Angela so that Jenkins could get a promotion.

'It's gotta go through Jones. He's the one hands out the cameras.'

'But you gave yours away.'

'I got something, some hush-hush project on. Can't say what. But I got no time for all this.'

'You haven't found a miracle?'

'Can't say.'

'Have you? You have!'

Jenkins was such an idiot. 'No, listen. It's not that. Jenkins, don't go gossiping. I've got a secret, unrelated project I'm working on. It means I haven't got time for Jones and his cameras. But don't go saying anything. OK?'

Hopefully by the time Delilah went round to Joanna Jones's house, he'd be in Cornwall with Angela. Otherwise this joke was going to go sour very soon.

'No, I see.' Jenkins tried to look very secretive and trustworthy, which had the opposite effect of suggesting that the next time Lucas saw him, Jenkins might very well be wearing a T-shirt emblazoned with *Guess who found a miracle?* and a pointy-fingered hand which would allow Jenkins to stand next to Lucas and align himself so the finger was pointing towards him.

'You travel all over, with the cats?' Lucas asked him.

'Yes.'

'You go outside London?'

'Very occasionally.'

'You got a special pass?'

Jenkins understood that this was the payback for the info about how to get ahead in the Ministry by prostituting his wife on camera. But still, a pass outside of London was a big deal. He was going to make Lucas work for it.

'See, I got to get outside London because of this project. I need a pass. I was thinking of asking Jones.'

'He can't help you.'

'No.'

'You got to fill in endless forms.'

'I know. And I don't want to do that – it's a secret, see. Listen, Jenkins. I'm serious. Don't tell anyone. I shouldn't even tell you but, well, I trust you. You know?'

'It is a miracle, isn't it?'

He was silent. Jenkins took his silence for agreement. He was so excited, perhaps he would also take to wearing a comedy *Guess who found a miracle* hat with the T-shirt. He could get them printed in bulk and distributed to relatives. Delilah could wear one while she was doing her sex show with Joanna Jones.

'I can't believe it,' Jenkins said. He clearly did believe it.

'If I had found a miracle – and I'm not saying I have – it would take a long time to investigate and I'd need to get around outside of London to do it properly.'

'I've got passes for most of the territories in England, Scotland and Wales.'

'Pretty much everywhere, then?'

'Not Cornwall, Liverpool or Leeds.'

'Oh. Well, never mind. You got Devon?'

'Yes.'

Devon was next to Cornwall and getting close was better than nothing. They could do the rest alone. He'd bribe the border guards. He'd figure something out.

Through Jenkins's open door, Lucas saw Jones leave his office and walk down the corridor away from them.

Lucas spoke quietly. 'You been to Wales, Jenkins? Is it nice?'

'Yeah, I got family there. You know, people think this cats job isn't so good but I'm one of the few people gets to see my family, since the partition.'

'How about Delilah's family? You ever get to Ireland?'

'No. Matter of fact, she was trapped over here when the fences went up. Makes her pretty sad.'

'Come on,' Lucas said. 'I want to show you something.'

He led Jenkins into Jones's office. He felt sorry for Jenkins, with his family in Wales, his sad wife with her big frying pan hands and her donkey face. He wanted to warn Jenkins against the sick porno ring in the Ministry that, even though it was entirely of his own invention, disgusted him.

The office was empty. Jenkins was nervous. They went to the computer. Lucas nudged the keyboard, found the video player on the desktop. JJ. There she was. A lovely shot. She was in the kitchen, talking to the older woman with the jam who Lucas had met the other day. Jenkins was gobsmacked. He still had the camera equipment in his hands. Perhaps the fact that the older woman was sensible and unsexual reminded Jenkins of Delilah. He clearly suspected that here was a woman who had been sent to Jones's house for some hanky-panky. Lucas watched as the horror and shame of it hit Jenkins; he couldn't help looking, though he was repelled by it.

They left the office. Jenkins was silent. Lucas could tell by the way he was carrying it that Jenkins didn't want the camera equipment any more. They went to Jenkins's office and Jenkins looked out some passes for Lucas. Drinking Ribena in Jones's office was never going to have the same thrill for Jenkins, if he ever did it again.

On Jenkins's desk there was a photo of a woman who didn't look like a donkey. She had dark hair and high cheekbones and a smiling face. Delilah, presumably. Lucas looked at the photo and then looked at Jenkins. Jenkins saw him looking. Lucas smiled at Jenkins. Jenkins looked away.

So now he had passes which would take him as far as Devon, at least. He was sorry he'd had fun at Jenkins's expense. He'd demeaned both of them by it. Perhaps he could make amends by being kind to someone; time to go and have another look at Christina, the little miracle child.

He went down to the lobby in the lift, went to his car, got into it and drove away from the Ministry. As he drove he wondered, if he had secret cameras installed at home now, what would they show? He had no idea what Angela did all day. When he asked her, she just said 'nothing much' or 'I made a cake' or 'I made a fish stew.' Perhaps, if she was lonely, he ought to introduce her to Delilah Jenkins, although not in a 'home video' way. The woman had a nice face. She and Angela could be friends. But he was going to take Angela to Cornwall. It would be just as well if she didn't make any new friends, he didn't want her confiding in anyone and ruining their plans. Besides, Jenkins would never stand for it. He'd think there were cameras installed at the house and Delilah was showing her arse to the men at the Ministry without any chance of a promotion in it for him.

He was almost at Maureen and Christina's house when he decided, on a whim, to go home and surprise Angela and see for himself what she did all day when he wasn't there. Why hadn't he ever thought of doing that before? Why didn't he go home and have lunch with her every day? Because he had work to do. But still.

He parked in one of those chichi little villagey streets that used to make London such a nice place to live, and he went into a flower shop. There was a time when flower shops, cake shops, beauticians and so on were places where you'd be guaranteed to find a woman serving. Now it was always a man. It was good, in one way, because there was no unemployment. But it might have been nice to go into a flower shop and see a woman in one of those nylon aprons putting together a bouquet. Today, there would be a gay man behind the counter – he was so sure if it, he wouldn't even bother taking a bet with himself – and the bouquet would be done with good taste and the man would be called Kevin, and he'd try to steer the choice of bouquet towards something tasteful, when actually Lucas wanted something scented and gorgeous and ludicrously over the top to take home for Angela.

The bell jangled as he went into the shop. The man behind the counter was wearing one of those green cotton aprons that men barbecue in. He wasn't especially gay or experimental in attitude or appearance, which was slightly disappointing. The man made up an extraordinary bouquet of towering spikes of scented and non-scented English flowers: phlox, snapdragons, foxgloves, delphiniums, roses. Lucas felt emotional when he looked at it, which surprised him. Was it the Englishness of it when England, as such, didn't exist any more? Was it only because he was buying a gift for Angela and it reminded him how much he loved her?

'What's your name?' he asked the man in the green apron. He still had a soppy expression on his face from admiring the flowers. The man looked at him as if he was the gay one.

'Arthur.'

'Those flowers are lovely, Arthur. Very English, like your name. Like seasides and countrysides.'

'Long time since either of us have seen the sea, I'll bet.'

'You can go down to the sand on the Thames at low tide, near London Bridge. Have you seen them do it?'

The trouble with asking questions of strangers was that they were often wary of you, especially if you drew up outside their place of work in a Ministry car with tinted windows. But Arthur responded openly, if perhaps a little too respectfully: 'Yes. Not the same though, is it, sir? That saltiness in the air as you lick your ice cream. The sound of the waves, kids laughing, sand castles, going home to put on after-sun cream.' He didn't say whether he'd seen it on a documentary on TV or whether he remembered these things from his childhood. He was older than Lucas, perhaps he remembered it.

Lucas took the flowers and the scent almost overwhelmed him. He could have stood there and cried, looking at the man, Arthur, with his English name, his not-especially gay attitude to floristry and his distant memories of a better life, when people had thought nothing of going to the seaside and buying ice creams for their kids.

'Lucky lady,' said Arthur. 'Your wife, is it? Or girlfriend?'

'My wife. She's pregnant.'

'Oh, lovely. When?'

Did Arthur want to know when she had got pregnant? Was that the sort of thing that people asked when you announced the news? How intrusive and awful. He gawped at Arthur, horrified. Should he say 'a month ago' or would that be considered too early to go about telling strangers?

'When's it due?' prompted Arthur.

'Oh. Um…'

'Do you know what it is yet?' Arthur said, as if determined to get through the allocated list of questions florists were supposed to ask prospective fathers, irrespective of whether Lucas answered them or not. 'Or is it a surprise?'

'A girl.'

Arthur ducked down behind the counter and came up with a very small pink teddy bear, which he waved in the air as if Lucas was a child and they were playing a game. With two hands needed to hold the bouquet, Lucas couldn't take hold of the toy. The only solution was for

Arthur, with a tailor's efficiency, to tuck the pink teddy into one of Lucas's pockets.

Arthur held the door open so Lucas could go to his car.

'Goodbye, Arthur.'

Arthur looked at Lucas as if he knew that he'd been lying about everything. 'Goodbye, sir,' he said.

Lucas drove home with the bouquet buckled into the passenger seat next to him, that's how large it was. It was a bouquet a man would only buy for his wife if he was guilty about something. Lucas had never bought Angela anything so extravagant before, even for her birthday.

He wished he would go home and she'd tell him that she was pregnant. He'd produce the flowers and say, 'I know.' He'd know because of the way they'd made love the particular day it had happened, the way she'd looked at him, something about her body and the way it had seemed softer in the last few days.

He'd give her the flowers and it would be the start of something. They'd thought that getting married was the start but this was the real thing; the three of them, another little life to care about. They'd sit down and make their plans to go to Cornwall. He'd be especially solicitous of her. He'd make her a cup of tea, get her a hot water bottle, rub her back. He'd run her a bath. He'd pull some of the petals from the roses in the bouquet and strew them in the bath for her (would he? Or would that make her cross because it would spoil the bouquet? He wasn't sure how to proceed on that one.) She'd take off all her clothes and sit in the bath with her knees up and

111

lots of bubbles the way they had it in films, and she'd talk to him. Then he'd make dinner and she'd fiddle about in the kitchen, singing. She'd come and stand behind him and nuzzle him and he'd feel her heartbeat against his back, and maybe the baby's heartbeat. Then he realised he was imagining himself in one of those green barbecuing aprons that Arthur had been wearing. They didn't even have an apron like that. Arthur was intruding into his perfectly legitimate and lovely baby announcement fantasy. It made him cross. It put him in a slightly bad mood as he drew up outside the house and went in.

Angela wasn't there. He called out her name. He expected to find her singing or in the bath or whatever women did when the men weren't at home. The house was silent, not even any music playing. He cocked his head and listened. He put the bouquet on the table, very carefully, so the stems and flowers wouldn't be damaged.

He touched the kettle and it was cold. He went upstairs.

The spare bedroom was the first room he came to at the top of the stairs. It was empty. Next, the bathroom. He pushed the door open and looked inside. There was a rumpled-up T-shirt and a pair of white knickers with blood on them on the floor. He was overwhelmed with terror. Someone – Jones? – had been here and raped his wife. Someone had hurt her. They had cut her with a knife or raped her or hurt her so much, they'd made her bleed. He picked up the discarded clothes and looked at them. The T-shirt didn't give anything away but there was definitely fresh blood on her knickers. He flung the clothes down, started gasping for breath, gasping. He couldn't see. Was it a panic attack? He was blinded by tears. Where had they taken her?

He went to their bedroom, expecting the worst, but she wasn't there. He blundered about the house, looking for clues. Was she dressed or undressed? Had they bundled her, naked–

The front door opened and closed. Footsteps. He wiped his nose and eyes with the back of his hands. If only he had a gun. Tomorrow, if he lived, he would buy a gun.

'Hello?' It was her voice, puzzled. 'Hello? Lucas?'

She came upstairs. 'Lucas? Are you alright? What's the matter?'

She hadn't been hurt. There was something, some reason why he'd known all along she was alright. But he couldn't put his finger on it. What was wrong with him? What was happening? He went from the bedroom into the bathroom. He ran the cold tap, washed his face.

'Lucas?'

He stared up at her, like a guilty child, his eyes red from crying. 'Hay fever,' he said. She'd have seen the flowers.

'Oh God, you're in an awful state. They're so beautiful, those flowers. Are they from you?'

'Yes.'

She saw the T-shirt and the knickers on the floor. She picked them up, embarrassed. 'I didn't expect you home. Are you sure you're alright, Lucas?'

'I thought you'd been hurt.'

'I had to go to Fiona's next door for tampons. Sorry. I didn't mean to upset you. I didn't expect you back.'

'I thought you might be pregnant, this time.'

She winced a bit. He was sitting on the loo, seat down, staring at her. She had a cardboard box in a brown paper bag in her hand.

'Look, do you mind?' She waved the bag at him.

He did mind. He couldn't tell whether he minded more that she wasn't pregnant or that he was such an idiot that he was sitting on the toilet seat crying over a pair of knickers streaked with menstrual blood.

He got up, went downstairs, left her to it.

He wondered if she was on the pill and hadn't said anything about it. The thing about birth control was that a woman was supposed to have her husband's permission to use it. It was for her protection. It was something to do with rapists, paedophiles or terrorists – everything was, these days. It was the same with alcohol. Women weren't supposed to drink it without their husband's permission. That was to do with the rape laws, which were very complex. You'd rather be the Inspector of Cats than the Inspector of Rapists, that's for sure.

He wondered if she wanted a cat. He wasn't even sure if she wanted a baby. Should he tackle her about being on the pill? He could offer her a cat and then catch her off guard and ask about contraception. If he said it was against the law to take it without his permission, she'd laugh at him. He ought to look, work out her hiding place, if she had one.

If he still had the cameras, he could install them, not to spy on her naked, just to check that she wasn't taking birth control pills. That wasn't a betrayal. That was just checking that she wasn't betraying him, which was different.

He got some food out of the fridge, to make dinner. She came downstairs and separated the flowers into three small bouquets and put them in vases.

'Thank you for my flowers,' she said. She came and stood behind him and cuddled him. It was the way he'd imagined it except that he wasn't dressed in a green apron like Arthur and she wasn't pregnant.

She offered to help with the cooking but he didn't let her. She took an ibuprofen tablet, sat on a chair, hugged herself and winced. He chopped vegetables and took no notice. If she was pregnant, he'd have made her a cup of tea or something.

'Would you like a cat?'

'Hmm?'

'I could get you a cat?'

'Flowers, a cat – you're overwhelming me with presents today. What have I done?'

He carried on chopping. A green apron like Arthur's would be handy for when he did the cooking, actually. Otherwise your trousers got spattered and you went about smelling of onions.

'Have you done something you're not telling me, Lucas?'

'Huh?'

'Well, flowers, kittens, that little teddy bear – is that for me?'

The teddy bear was still sticking out of his pocket. She couldn't have the fucking teddy bear if she wasn't pregnant, that's for sure. Arthur had given it to him for their baby.

'It's for Christina.'

'The disabled girl?'

'Yes.'

'That's sweet.'

She took the teddy bear out of his pocket and she put it on the table, propping it up next to one of the vases of flowers. He wasn't sure how to ask her about the birth control. He'd just have to come out with it.

'You know they've got all sorts of different birth control pills now.'

'What do you mean?' She sounded very sharp.

'Christina – she'll be on birth control, won't she?'

'What on earth are you on about?'

'Paedophiles. Imagine if she got pregnant.'

'For Christ's sake, Lucas. Are you wondering if I'm on the pill, is that it?'

'I was thinking about Christina. I'm on my way to visit her in a minute.' He wasn't. But the detail added authenticity to the line of questioning, he felt.

'But it's dinner time.'

'Do you take the pill, then?'

'You're saying it's my fault I'm not pregnant? You want to divorce me and marry some little fourteen-year-old and get her pregnant instead? Imagine some fourteen-

116

year-old child trying to give birth to your big baby with its big head stuck in her cunt. No wonder so many of them die in childbirth.'

Angela said cunt? Maybe she was upset. Maybe she wanted to get pregnant and she was upset about it. He hadn't thought of that. He put down the vegetable knife and washed the smell of onion off his hands as best he could. Then he went and sat down next to her. He stroked her hair and kissed her face. She closed her eyes. A tear trickled down from one eye. He hoped it was the onions that were making her cry.

'Angela?'

She didn't say anything. What should he do to cheer her up? He'd already given her flowers. He was cooking her dinner. He couldn't give her that teddy because he'd said it was meant for a disabled child.

'Why don't you come and see Christina with me? You'll like her. I told her about your singing.'

'Did you?'

She was pleased about that.

'We'll have some dinner and then we'll go.'

Right, so now he was taking his wife to see a child who was not going to be declared a miracle, against all official rules and policy. He'd spent a lot of money on flowers. He hadn't got an answer about the birth control. He didn't know whether to feel sorry for Angela or himself or both of them. He didn't know anything. But then he went to bed pretty much every night feeling that, so tonight would be no different. One thing he was sure about, though, he was going to start being more honest, less reckless. He'd get them to Cornwall and then their problems would sort themselves out, most likely.

But at least Angela was more cheerful. She sat there and wrinkled up her face and tapped her finger on her lips. He could see that she was casting around for a lighter subject for them to talk about. There wasn't much to choose from: his work, her day, what was for dinner. She came up with something, though. Jesmond.

There was no way she could be allowed to know what had happened. He had to protect her. 'He hasn't been back here, has he?' So much for being more honest.

'No.'

'He's such a phoney.' His voice was crackly as he said it, like a gramophone record played by old people remembering their youth in a scene in a really bad film on TV.

Talking about Jesmond was like some awful test, to see if he could still deny he loved the man, even knowing he was dead. He now saw with horrible clarity that, as he was affected by Jesmond's death, the sneering attitude he'd always adopted must simply have been a mask, a way of protecting himself from admitting he cared about the man in case he disappeared like so many others of his generation. But he had to keep up with the sneering, otherwise Angela would suspect something had happened to Jesmond and ask about it.

'He believes in something,' she said. 'That book of his...'

Lucas thought about Jesmond, his complexion highly coloured and veiny like a pink geranium, his hair longish and curly like a Beethoven wig. He wished Jesmond was standing in front of Angela, book in hand, declaiming his awful poetry. Women loved that sort of thing. Poor old Jesmond.

'I wondered what you knew about him.'

'What do you mean?'

'About his personal life?'

'I don't know anything.'

'Didn't your dad ever tell you stories about when they used to go around together?'

'He took it upon himself to be Poet Laureate for a united England without ever being invited by anyone to fill that role,' Lucas said. He recited a phrase at random from *This Faerie England*, from memory: 'This colossal opportunity to build a new community…'

'Don't take the piss.'

'So far as I know,' Lucas said, 'he was a reprobate and a shagger and a drunk. My dad didn't say much to me about Jesmond before he died – and obviously he hasn't said anything to me about anything at all, since.'

'Your dad's not the only one, Lucas. I miss my dad, too.'

Lucas put on some music and they ate their dinner in silence, without hostility, preoccupied with their own thoughts. Both were thinking about Jesmond. If they had only known it, they might have been able to bring some comfort to each other.

Angela wondered if Lucas had somehow sensed that she had formed this 'relationship' with Jesmond through his letters, and that he was jealous. She cheered up at the thought that she might be able to persuade Jesmond to start writing to her – not as a lover but as a correspondent, a friend – next time he dropped round to the house.

Lucas looked over at Angela and regretted asking about the contraceptive pills. What was it he had heard somewhere? Never ask a question you don't know the answer to. It was the sort of wise advice that only came back to you after the event. He wished he could say it was the sort of advice he was always getting from his dear old dad. But his dear old dad had been a waster and a drunkard. Angela might kick against it sometimes and complain and grumble. But it was a wonder he had turned out as well as he had.

'Maybe we should talk about our parents,' Angela said as they were getting ready to go out.

'Maybe we should,' he said. But then he started brushing his teeth with ostentatious, foaming vigour, as if she should take her turn first.

'I know what you think of your dad but you never talk about your mum.'

He spat the toothpaste into the sink and wiped a finger round his mouth to make sure there was no white residue on his face – so unattractive, even between married couples. He said, 'She was a woman who believed in possibilities.'

He moisturised, looking at himself in the mirror while he smoothed the cream on in gentle, upward strokes, as directed by the manufacturer. Angela came and stood right next to him and looked into the eyes of the mirror version of him.

'That's it? That's all you've got to say?'

'You think talking about her's a way of keeping her alive?'

'I wondered what she was really like.'

'I've got the newspaper clippings, I'll show you.'

'Yeah. Cool.'

'She was one of those, she put her life into her art and she thought you should put art into your life. You know?'

Angela didn't know. How could she? 'I wish I'd seen some of her work. Was it all confiscated?'

'I don't know what happened to it. The last thing she worked on was something she called the Possibilities Project. You should read the articles, some of them would make you puke. She's always "crisply attractive". Or "sexily enigmatic". They'll mention her cheekbones, her hairstyle, the swish of her skirt. They pay too much attention to how she looked and not enough to what she thought.'

'She was beautiful, though. Those photos of her downstairs with your dad. She really was lovely to look at. I bet when they came to interview her, she knocked them out.'

'Trouble is, you get a woman who's intelligent and interesting and beautiful, people get seduced by that. Then some others react against it and get jealous.'

'You ever wish you were famous, Lucas?'

'How would I know if I was? Where are the newspapers to print articles about it? There's only the underground press. Nothing on TV except old films and nature documentaries.'

'I suppose you'd know because you'd get recognised on the street. People would tell stories about you. Sing your songs if you wrote them.'

Jesmond! Why couldn't she leave it?

'Yeah. Well then, I definitely don't wish I was famous.'

'I wouldn't mind being known for some sort of achievement.'

'Better buy a printing press and start a newspaper if you want a mention.'

'You know what I mean.'

Lucas hadn't thought the day could get any worse but now all of a sudden Angela was interested in making something of her life.

14   No Goatee

Jason Prince would have liked to grow a goatee beard. He suspected it would have sharpened his chin and made him look more intelligent. But he couldn't really do that, he had to be clean-shaven, out of solidarity with the girls. Still, he sometimes stroked the area on his chin where a goatee might have been. He believed it helped him think.

Jason was thinking about the people in the club the night Jesmond was killed, and which of them might have been spies. Unfortunately, it was like April Fool's Day; as soon as he remembered it was April 1st, everything everyone said or did on that day seemed absurd, and now the more he thought about it, the more likely it seemed that anyone in the club might have been a spy. But surely the audience that night had only been made up of poets, poetry-lovers, artists and eccentrics. That old bat with the funny hat, for example, had looked properly old school, a performance artist with nowhere left to perform. The organisers had been taking a risk letting in someone who was so obviously a woman after the curfew, although there would have been several of them in the audience incognito. You got to recognise them after a while; their studied cowboy way of walking from side to side with shoulders high, legs apart and arms held wide, their jeans and black T-shirts too perfectly male, their faces too soft, their eyes too big, their chins too smooth.

He didn't blame himself for running when he came out of the club and saw what had happened to Jesmond. He had stepped over his hero's body and run away. After all, a vicious gang who had beaten one poet to death might easily have had enough rage left over to beat other poets. He hadn't wanted to hang around to find out, obviously. Others – either they were not poets or they were not cowards – had crouched around the body, checking for ID, a wallet or an item of jewellery to save and return to the family before the police arrived and dragged the body away. He doubted Jesmond had anything on him beyond his bus fare home. A life on the run made men cautious. It was, notoriously, one of the reasons why Jesmond had memorised his poems, so that there were no notebooks about his person with lyrics insisting that the reader should rise up, which would have given him away if he should ever have got stopped by the security forces or the police – although his face was so well-known, by now it must have been more a case of convention than prevention that made him travel so lightly.

Rise Up… Jason choked up at the memory of them all singing that song together that night. He felt he ought to try to do something to compensate for what those thugs had done to Jesmond. There was no question of him going after them, to get revenge. It would have been purposeless.

It wasn't even possible to determine who was responsible. It was probably nihilists. But because they claimed they didn't believe in anything, they didn't have symbols and insignia to identify themselves. This meant that when they carried out an atrocity, instead of spraying slogans or symbols around as calling cards, as other terrorists did, they left it to witnesses to work out who was responsible by a process of elimination. If no one else claimed it, it was probably nihilists. It was something of an insult, actually. If a person was going to be beaten to death, he would probably choose to be despatched by members of an organisation that stood for something, not by thugs who disdained even to choose a symbol to represent themselves.

Determined to do something to make amends for Jesmond's somewhat ignominious death, Jason went by bicycle to the address Jesmond had given him and watched the house, thinking that the occupants might lead him to Jesmond's family. He wasn't sure what he intended to do if he saw them. Apologise? Tell them what a great guy Jesmond had been, how wonderful that last night had been? No, because if he did so, it might almost seem that he was gloating at having been there.

Perhaps he was just being voyeuristic. Perhaps he secretly hoped that the family might come to the address he was watching to mourn, or that the occupants of this house would go somewhere and meet up with other famous writers to celebrate Jesmond's death, and he might feel connected to them all somehow, by watching them. Was he really only hanging around in hope of seeing famous people? He had to believe he wasn't. Actually, so far as he was aware, all the other famous writers had long since gone to live in exile, or had been detained. Jesmond had been the last one left.

Jason leaned the pedal of his bike against the kerb and sat with his buttocks resting on the saddle, one foot on the ground and one foot on the kerb, and he waited. And from time to time, he stroked his chin, approximately in the region where his goatee might have been, if he'd had one.

He liked the look of the house. It was a white-painted 1930s villa, semi-detached, with a tidy front garden and a little stone path leading from the gate up to the house. There were peonies growing in the borders. The place was modest, attractive, not like some of the houses in the street, with their gardens crammed full of ostentatious ornaments. People had so little to spend their money on – foreign holidays were out, for example. They didn't have to pay to put their parents or grandparents in nursing homes as most died long before they became too frail to cope. Almost no one was a saver, when the future was so uncertain. Londoners were spenders and he could hardly criticise them for that, although he sometimes found it difficult to understand why they felt they had to spend their money on such gaudy tat.

After he had been watching the house for about an hour, he saw a woman come out of the house in her veil and covers. She looked young, the way she carried herself. Her frame was slight. Jason was ready to follow but she only went up to the door of the neighbouring house, knocked on the door and went inside.

About half an hour after that bit of excitement, Jason was surprised to see a Ministry car turn up at the house. Very surprised. Frightened, even. Maybe they had come to cart off the occupants? He watched as a smooth-looking man got out of the car holding a bunch of expensive-looking flowers. He was one of those confident types with movie-star looks, well-groomed, a year or two older than Jason. Perhaps the flowers were to break the news of Jesmond's death. Perhaps the woman inside was Jesmond's wife or daughter. But then why the Ministry car? A known link to Jesmond would be dangerous for a Ministry man. Maybe that's why this was a safe house for Jesmond; it was a bluff. No one would ever think the respectable people inside actually passed messages along to Jesmond or helped him. Then again, maybe they hadn't helped Jesmond. Maybe it was they who had dobbed him in.

Could Jesmond himself have been a spy, a tool of the establishment, used as a focus for discontent, so that those who were inclined towards revolution could be weeded out? Had Jesmond been the cheese in the mousetrap of the establishment? He thought it over and he thought not. Jesmond had been the real deal.

While he waited, Jason thought of writing a poem, provisionally entitled *The flowers that he brought you*. The good thing about being a poet was that you could spend your time sitting around, thinking, and every phrase that popped into your head was potentially useful. So even a long afternoon spent watching someone's house with the pointed end of a saddle working its way into your arse crack could seem fairly productive.

Considering how many thoughts a man must have in a day, it was odd that he wasn't more prolific. But poetry was about quality, not quantity. He thought, he sifted, he used or discarded. It would be nice to just lie down and think, his head on his arm, his eyes closed, and have someone else record his thoughts for him. Saying them aloud wouldn't work. He had no use for a Dictaphone or any instrument like that. He was interested in the thoughts as they floated in his head before they became speech. The process of converting the words into speech was just one more method of sifting and selecting them. He liked to access the thoughts before they reached that stage, when they were all wandering around inside his head like sheep on a hillside.

Thus he spent a lovely afternoon thinking about how he thought, and marvelling at the process, as if no one else in the whole history of the world had ever had a head full of thoughts. He was well-intentioned enough, though. And if young men never sat about thinking how brilliant they were, then precious little would ever get written, so if he ever got old and he looked back on this day and other days like it, he wasn't going to feel too angry with himself.

After a while, the young woman in the veil and covers emerged from her neighbour's house carrying a brown paper bag. Her eyes seemed to catch his for a moment but she looked down at the pavement and continued with the short journey back to her own home.

Jason wanted to say something in the poem about hope. Something about beauty and hope and making a connection with another person. He would have liked to mention the peonies, but there was something too much like *pee on me* about the sound of the word, although the flowers themselves were beautiful, like soft roses. Gauzy roses? Perhaps he could do something with gauzy.

You exhale slowly, sorrowfully
A puff of breath, the gauzy veil
lifts temporarily
Our eyes connect

No. That wouldn't do. He'd try again when he got home. He often took his inspiration from mundane events but he didn't consider it his duty to document them. It amused him the way some people thought that poets only talked about real events, meticulously setting down what had actually happened, as if poetry was written under caution. When he wrote poetry, he tried to be truthful. But not in the way that people imagined. Almost the best thing about being a poet was that, no matter what kind of day he'd had, how tiresome or tedious, he would have noticed something, or a few lines would have formed in his head that he could later use, and he'd be able to say to himself at the end of it, 'At least I got a poem out of it.'

Presently, he saw a nondescript man walking hurriedly along the pavement, looking this way and that. He looked very shifty. Jason turned his face away but the man wasn't interested, he was too busy worrying about who might be looking at *him*. He stopped at the little white gate leading to the house Jason was watching, trotted up to the door and posted a slip of paper through the letterbox. It might have been a flyer or something like that, which was nothing unusual, except that he didn't deliver to any of the other houses in the street. Perhaps he was a gaudy tat merchant who'd noticed how poorly-served this house was for such material, and had seen an opportunity to make a buck. Or not.

The nondescript man had the androgynous look of a person who might enjoy going to underground poetry events. He might have been one of the men who'd searched Jesmond's body for ID after the poetry event. But then again, maybe not. Everyone did their best to look the same as everyone else these days, not drawing attention to themselves or standing out in a crowd. Jason couldn't very well shout over and ask if he was a poetry aficionado as it was against the law to congregate in clubs at night and listen to people speaking out against the authorities, even if they did it prettily, in verse. A question like that was tantamount to an accusation and could lead to trouble if put to the wrong person. As it was, the man turned and went back the way he had come, so Jason didn't get a proper look at him and the man never got a look at Jason's face, either. If he had, maybe he would have recognised him. Maybe not.

Jason waited a while longer but there was no sign of anyone else coming to the house, or anyone leaving. To be honest, he was slightly wary in case that ministry man came out of his house, saw Jason and thought he'd put that note through his letterbox, whatever it was. Better not risk a misunderstanding. It seemed that he would have to leave and return to his spy duties the following day.

He wondered how he should go about getting safe passage for someone if he wanted to help them leave London. He'd heard of people who'd planned to leave, who'd paid huge sums of money to traffickers. He'd subsequently heard that they had left. Unfortunately no one ever seemed to know whether those people had come out safely at the other end. Still, if the occupants of this pleasant suburban house should lead him to Jesmond's family, he thought he would do all he could for them, including making enquiries about how they could find safe passage out of London. What did he have to lose? Even at his young age, he had more than enough money than he would ever be able to spend in his lifetime; he doubted he would live as long as Jesmond. There was something rather funny about minding so much about an old man dying, when so many much younger men did not survive. But perhaps it was his longevity that made it so sad. Jesmond was a venerable old geezer and he had survived this long, so it would have been much more fitting if he had simply died in his sleep after a heavy night on the vino.

Jason went home to see how much cash he could lay his hands on. He would ask around in dodgy places run by foreigners trapped in London after partition; the sort who went out of their way to maintain their separateness from other Londoners, as if it might count in their favour if ever the fences came down and the citizens of London were put on trial for their conduct towards each other. He went to the rooms above cafés run by Turkish people that he had heard you should visit for illegal transactions such as these, the sleazy men-only nightclubs in Soho run by Greeks, the men-only cinemas run by the Welsh, the transport companies run by Albanians and Scots. He would visit every mythically low-life venue he had ever heard of, and he would beg and bargain and plead, and somehow or other he would contrive to buy a family their freedom.

But first, he had to find the family he wanted so desperately to help. So the next day – and the next day, and the day after that, if need be – he would come back to the pleasant 1930s villa and watch it, see where the occupants went and who visited them, and try to determine who among them might be Mrs Jesmond and the junior Jesmond(s), if such people even existed.

15 From Beyond the Grave

She didn't dare tell Lucas but this afternoon, shortly after he came home unexpectedly and made a scene, she'd heard the flap on the letterbox open and then close again, quietly. Perhaps she'd heard footsteps walking away from the house or perhaps that's just what she would have expected to hear. She'd thought absolutely nothing of it; another pizza delivery leaflet, another menu from a local curry house. She'd pick it up and recycle it next time she went past the front door, just as she did with all the others.

But when she went to pick up the piece of paper from the doormat, she was astonished by what she saw. It was a poem, handwritten, with her address at the bottom. She opened the door and looked out, as if he might still be there, even though he must have been out of sight by then.

Jesmond couldn't have known that Lucas had burned his journal and his letters. He couldn't have known that she had been reading them and that, without them, and without knowing what had happened between him and the woman he loved, she was feeling bereft. It was absurd to think that he had written the poem and brought it here for her and then, at the last minute, that perhaps he had been too shy or too nervous to ring the doorbell because he had sensed her growing affection for him. She knew he couldn't have sensed anything of the sort. No doubt he hadn't rung the doorbell because he'd seen Lucas's car outside and couldn't face another cold welcome. When he turned up, it was often in the daytime, when he knew he'd find Angela at home alone and could be sure of a polite chat and a meal. But perhaps his nerve had failed him this time.

While Lucas was upstairs changing his shirt for their visit to Christina, she looked again at the poem. It must be another piece for 'the archive'. But still, she couldn't shake the idea that he had written it just for her and crept up to the door and dropped it through the letterbox to console her for the loss of the letters.

She studied the piece of paper the poem was written on. The handwriting didn't look the same as the writing on the letters. But then she had been reading the writing of a man twenty years younger. Perhaps he had written this one in a hurry, in a hand that had matured. Certainly, the poetry seemed to have matured. It seemed superior to Jesmond's greatest hits, although maybe that was just because they were over-familiar and she took them for granted, like Beatles songs.

The poem, 'her' poem, didn't seem to be revolutionary, it was a love song. It was rather solemn, like a hymn. She read it and she felt the tears start to come. She couldn't have said whether it was because she was happy or sad. She had that shivery comforted feeling that came with redemptive happy endings, like learning that someone she cared about cared about her, or that Bambi's mother hadn't died after all, that sort of feeling. But she had never before cried because she was happy, so most likely she was crying now because she was sad.

She heard Lucas coming down the stairs. She stopped crying and picked up her handbag and found a tissue in it and blew her nose. She took a bottle of perfume from a pocket inside the bag and dabbed a bit of it on her wrists and on the hollow at the base of her neck at the front, just above her collarbone. She put the perfume back in the pocket in the bag and tucked the poem in next to it. She turned away to the mirror and touched up her lipstick while Lucas put his shoes on, then they went outside and got into the car with the tinted windows and he drove them to Maureen's house. By the time they got there, both were sufficiently recovered. It would have been difficult to tell that they had spent most of the latter part of the day crying, independently of each other, off and on.

16   Taking Charge

Maureen looked like shit. Lucas was surprised. OK, so she hadn't been expecting them. But it was as if someone had set fire to her since the last time he'd seen her. And that didn't mean that she was sparking and sizzling. It meant she looked like she had been reduced to a pile of ash. She was grey. She was smaller. Maybe Delilah Jenkins had been round and banged her upside the head with a frying pan. That's how she looked. She didn't even seem to recognise him. Why oh why hadn't he called to tell her he'd be coming and that he'd be bringing his wife?

'Maureen? It's me. Are you OK?' You look like shit.

Maybe the kid had died. Maybe the house had been burgled and someone had robbed all her stuff and raped the kid. That's how she looked.

'I'm so sorry. I wasn't expecting you.'

'We can come back. Don't worry.'

'Is that your wife?'

'Yes, this is Angela.'

136

'Oh, do come in. He said he might bring you but I never… people say it but they never mean it. How kind of you to come. How kind of you. Please come in.'

They went in. She tried to get them to eat some cake but they explained they had just eaten. Angela was very curious. He realised it was because she didn't get out much and this was a great adventure for her. She didn't normally even go out after dark. She'd seemed a bit jittery on the way here in the car. But now she looked around as if she wanted to remember every inch of Maureen's home so they could discuss it afterwards. In future, he'd tell her about the places he visited, in the kind of detail she was taking in now. He did talk about his work, of course. He'd generally tell her a bit about the people, whether he liked them or not, what type of miracle they were reporting, his reaction (if it seemed witty to him): 'Well, I'm sorry, Mrs So-and-So, but it's clear to me that you're the one who arranged those pieces of red pepper in that flan to look like Father Christmas. It's a talent but it's not a miracle.' That sort of thing.

He saw her looking at Maureen's house and realised he should have been telling her the colour of the paintwork, the pictures on the wall, what the women were wearing. That was what she was looking at now.

Maureen said, 'Would you like to see Christina?'

Of course they would. He had tried to explain to Angela – he was at great pains to make sure she understood it – that this was not a miracle. He was only bringing her here because he felt sorry for the child and he had told the child's mother that his wife could sing. So she wasn't to get excited and expect too much. How often had he thought about discovering a miracle and keeping it for them both? Did she know? Did she suspect? But this wasn't it. This wasn't a miracle.

'She's awake,' Maureen said. 'I was just reading her a story.'

They went into the room where the child was kept. There she was, hair all shiny and brushed, lying in bed.

'There,' said Maureen. 'She smiled. Did you see it? She only does that for people she likes.'

Angela went over to the bed, grasped Christina's hand and stared at the little creature, right in the eyes.

'Yes,' she said. 'Yes, I saw it. Hello, Christina. How are you, lovely girl?'

She turned her hand over and drew the backs of her fingers very, very softly along the child's cheek, then down her arm, then across her bony hand.

'Isn't she adorable?' Angela said to Lucas. The child didn't look awful but she didn't look particularly adorable, so he assumed she'd said it for Maureen's benefit.

'Hmm,' he said. 'Oh yes.'

It was a bit odd, the way Angela was taking charge. It was as if she'd brought him to see Christina and not the other way around. He tried to imagine what it would be like if women had jobs. What if a woman was the boss? He couldn't imagine it, actually. What must have it been like, before? Were there women in Australia now in charge of banks or government departments or newspapers, ordering men about? Smelling nice and taking charge like this?

He was just thinking what an awful idea this whole thing was when Angela began to sing. She sat next to Christina and held her hand and looked into her eyes as if she was in love with her, and she began to sing. He and Maureen couldn't help themselves, they exchanged a blissful look.

Angela had a lovely voice. Did a man always think his wife had a lovely voice, the way he always thought his wife had a prettier face than other men's wives? Perhaps. Maureen wasn't married to Angela but she seemed to admire her voice. Her sad old sooty face looked like a marshmallow melting on a bonfire; sweet and sad and ruined. She began to cry. Stop it, Maureen, he thought. You'll make me cry. Stop it. It was as if a cartoon villain had squirted crying juice all over the place. He jabbed a pen lid into the palm of his hand and thought about genocide, and that pulled him up a bit. The death of millions, paraded in his imagination to stop him making a fool of himself in front of Maureen. Hopefully it was not the case that by airing such memories, he somehow made the people suffer again in some slight way – the shadows and ghosts of the people. No, he'd never heard that theory expounded. His father had considered himself something of a philosopher when he was drunk and he liked to sing Irish folk tunes but he never gave advice and he never gave voice to the theory that memories damage the people who are remembered. Shame, or he would remember his own father more. Ha!

Angela looked at him. She seemed to be expecting him to say something. Had she just asked him a question?

'I love to hear you sing.'

'But did you see her smile?'

'Who?'

'Christina.'

'I'm not sure.'

'You were day-dreaming again.'

Maureen was overcome. Angela gave her a hug. They stood and rocked together, Angela's arms around Maureen, deeply emotional. He realised he wasn't used to seeing women together. Was this how Maureen had carried on when she had worked for the television news? He hoped not.

But if Maureen wanted to cry and hug a stranger, well, OK. Life must be pretty tough for her. What was there to lose by letting her take comfort in Angela's singing?

17 Anna Gray

While Angela was in the shower the next morning, Lucas had a quick look through her underwear drawer. He had seen her slip a piece of paper into it from her handbag. It looked as though it had a poem written on it and he thought it likely she had palmed it from the journal he had burnt. If she was guarding it closely, it meant he didn't need to worry too much from a security point of view; she probably wouldn't get careless and try to show it to anyone. Still, he probably ought to get rid of it.

He looked it over. It didn't seem to be subversive. It was a love song of some kind. It was written rather beautifully, actually. He allowed himself to dream, for a moment, that Angela had written it for him. But it was unlikely. It wasn't in her handwriting, for a start. He couldn't think of a reason she might have for dictating a love poem to someone else to write down – or not one that he could bear to think about.

He heard her come out of the bathroom. He was standing in the middle of the room in his underpants and, short of swallowing it, had nowhere to put the paper so that she wouldn't see him with it and know he'd taken it and intended to destroy it. Reluctantly, he put it back in the drawer. He'd deal with it later.

While she got dressed, he went downstairs and looked for the scrapbook his father had made with cuttings of newspaper articles about his mother and her work. As he flipped through the pages, he was surprised at how familiar they were, even though he hadn't looked at them for years, since his father died.

His mother had gone first. He hadn't understood it then. He'd thought she'd run away from them. His father had let him believe it for some reason. Perhaps he'd thought it was better that his son believed she was living elsewhere, making art, perhaps married to another man and bringing up another family, than that he should know the truth of what was going on all over London. But it happened so many times, to so many families, in the end he couldn't help but find out.

London was soon teeming with orphans, running the family home, in charge of the finances, eating what they wanted and going to bed late. Sales of computer games went up and academic results suffered. It was like one big exciting sleepover until the kids realised they had to make order out of the chaos, take care of siblings, get jobs, live carefully so they didn't get a visit from the police and get carted off. Those early years should have been wild with joyful anarchy but instead they became unbelievably bleak and everyone lived fearfully. Partly it was because those left behind were so young that they didn't understand the need to band together. They were inexperienced and they trusted the wrong people or they trusted no one. Acts of rebellion were mostly carried out by incautious individuals. Those who stood up and spoke out against the authorities were picked off. Those who remained learned quickly that it was better to keep their heads down and conform.

As he looked at the pages in the scrapbook, at his mother's smiling face in the photos illustrating articles about her in lifestyle magazines, leaning against a wall or in the doorway of one of the derelict places she had transformed by the power of her imagination, he couldn't help noticing the residual feelings of resentment that were still attached to his memories of her. She looked so elegant, resourceful, independent. She didn't look as if she needed to be the mother of a little boy to feel happy and successful. He could see, too, why the interviewers gushed when they met her. She was an attractive woman, and in every picture the camera seemed to have caught her just as she was about to leap up, brush the rest of the world aside – the camera, the art works, the banal trappings of everyday life – and reveal a secret that would astonish and amuse everyone who heard it, and give them no choice but to fall in love with her.

But perhaps he was just feeling the way every man felt when he saw photos of his mother when she was young. Who could he ask about that? Not Jones or Jenkins. He had no friends, only Angela, and he couldn't tell Angela how he felt. She might not understand.

Angela came up behind him and kissed him. She leaned around him to look at what he was looking at. Most of the articles in the scrapbook quoted Anna's explanations of her latest projects: *'Have you ever sat down and wondered how your life might have turned out if you'd made different choices? Of course you have. Have you ever sat down and wasted an afternoon following a strand all the way through that other life you could have had? Maybe not. But I have. Where would I have lived, who might I have married, what might I have achieved – or not achieved – if I had taken a different path, slept through a different afternoon, kissed a different man.'*

Angela read about how Anna had 'twinkled at', 'toyed with' and 'seemed wryly amused by' her interviewers while possibly (Angela thought) mocking them.

One article was illustrated with a photo of Anna leaning in a doorway, arms folded, smiling. Behind her was a picture she had painted, a trompe l'oeil which had transformed the space she'd been working in. The interviewer was obviously smitten: 'I'm looking at just one of many possible versions of the place the artist is standing in, one which she has created. And as I watch her pose for our photographer, I'm aware that I'm looking at just one version of all the possible versions of her, and I can't help wondering how I can find my way to a version of Anna Gray who might be persuaded to care for a man like me.'

Angela tapped her finger on the paragraph, to point it out to Lucas so he could read it.

'Eurggh,' he said.

'An artist who puts herself into her work,' Angela said, quoting from snippets in the scrap book that caught her eye. 'Blah blah, she often looks amused, as if sharing a joke... the transformation is what's important, the process doesn't matter... blah, blah blah... "The project might have had its germination in something we did when my son was small." Ah, listen to this Lucas: "We'd leave dog food out for hedgehogs and the foxes, nuts and seeds for the birds. Everyone does it, if they want to encourage wildlife in their garden and help them survive. And then I started to think about what you might do if you wanted to encourage *possibilities*. So I'd study these derelict or difficult places and go back to my studio and create alternative versions of them. At first I'd paint a picture and I'd bring a photograph of it back to the original place and leave it lying about, like evidence of a parallel world. Later on, I got more ambitious and tried to transform the original space. That's what I'm working on now. It's tough though, with these new restrictions on women going about the city.'"

Lucas looked at the pictures. 'Wherever she got to, I hope they appreciate her talents.'

'Somewhere with a theatre, maybe? She'd have made a terrific set designer,' said Angela. 'Oh, look at that one. That's nice.'

He suddenly felt rather irritable. He pointed out a paragraph in one of the interviews. Angela read it aloud: "'It's not a makeover project. It's not about leaving plastic flowers in a derelict building, although I have done that. It's not decorating. You understand? It's about exploring choices. It's political. You think if a man did this, people would say 'that's nice'? No. They'd ask about the intention behind it.'"

Angela blushed. Sometimes, for all the crap that went with living in London, it was a bonus not to have to put up with mothers-in-law. Popular literature suggested that they sniped and were critical of the women their sons married – and this one had even found a way to have a pop at Angela from beyond the grave.

Lucas saw that he had upset her and he was sorry. Of course she was jealous of his mother, she was bored. She needed something to occupy her. A hobby or something. A friend.

18   A Note from a Well-Wisher

And so it was that he spent the week ferrying Angela to Maureen's house every day on his way to work (with Jason in pursuit on his bicycle, though Lucas did not know it), so that Angela could sing to Christina and she and Maureen could hug each other in a womanly way (although not on camera).

On the way home every evening, he would pass by Maureen's house to collect Angela and be offered preposterous home-made cakes and biscuits; ginger snaps, garibaldi, and those squashed up dried fruit things with chocolate on the bottom, whatever they were. If he didn't eat enough of them while he was at the house – and it was difficult to know when he'd reached a limit she deemed suitable because Maureen was the only judge – then she would send him home with more of the stuff in a tin lined with greaseproof paper.

He somehow got into the habit of bringing little gifts to the house in return; a sparkly hair slide for Christina, a pot plant for Maureen. Small things, pretty, scented, lovely things that made Maureen almost crazily happily and caused her to remark how much he had made

Christina smile and she only did that when she really liked someone.

Maureen was the perfect mother figure for Angela. He heard her asking Maureen one day, as he was in the other room saying hello to Christina, had she ever heard of the Possibilities Project? Maureen said no. Then he heard her ask Maureen did she remember the artist Anna Gray. But Maureen said she was sorry, she couldn't recall the Possibilities Project or Anna Gray.

Having a famous person in the family, the rest of the family members were inclined to think other people must have heard of them, the way everyone always thinks other people know their secret, if they have one.

Maureen would have known Jesmond by name, of course, Angela didn't even have to ask. Who could forget a man who had set free all the animals in London zoo and then written a poem about it? Anyone who had ever seen a ring-tailed lemur squashed on the road or the glow of predatory eyes high up in a tree, or heard of another tiger getting shot as it emerged from Hyde Park to take a bite out of one of the shoppers going into Harrods, they couldn't help but bring Jesmond's name to mind.

One night, when Lucas came to collect Angela, Maureen showed them a note that had come through her door the night before, shortly after Lucas had collected Angela and taken her home. It was handwritten in blue ink. When she saw it, Angela's heart began to beat in an accelerated iambic metre. It was the same blue ink, the same handwriting as the poem Jesmond had put through her letterbox a couple of days earlier.

The message said:

If you want safe passage out of London, go down to Down Street. Keep going down. Then head for Heathrow. Take a toll for the trolls.
From a well-wisher.

There was a poem enclosed with the note, entitled Gauzy Love Song. Maureen said that phrases such as 'the merest puff' and 'a gentle exhalation' appeared to allude to Christina's illness and she thought the note might be from a paedophile.

'Get rid of it,' Lucas said.

'You think it's a trick?' Maureen asked him.

'It's gobbledygook.'

Angela was offended that Maureen had waited to show it to Lucas, unconsciously believing it was important to talk it over with a man first. No doubt Maureen felt she was an honorary man because she'd once had a job. Well, her time as a reporter hadn't done much to hone her investigative skills because Angela heard her admitting to Lucas that she was stumped, she had no idea what the note meant or who it was from. But Angela knew – it was meant for her. It was from Jesmond, who somehow understood that she had read some of those letters Lucas had destroyed and wanted to continue the correspondence.

Though she had no idea who it was from, the note had quite an effect on Maureen. She started to talk of leaving London. She talked of going to the countryside, somewhere remote, having picnics, walking with Christina to the top of a hill and rolling back down again, taking her shoes and socks off, paddling in streams.

This stirred Angela up. She forgot the mild animosity she'd felt towards Maureen at being excluded from discussions about the provenance of the note, and she talked of Australia and what they might do in that fine country, if only they could get there.

'You'd find help for Christina, Maureen,' she said. 'And I could get a job.'

Lucas tried to put a stop to their nonsense, as Angela talked of giving birth to her children in safety and comfort while attended by female midwives, of swimming in the ocean, of barbecues, equality, friendships.

'There's no way any of us would ever get to Australia. No way. As for "heading for Heathrow", what would be the point? There are no planes.'

'We could go by ship.'

'No, Angela. They chuck stowaways over the side when they find them. No one ever survives to tell the tale.'

'How do you know so much about it, then?'

As usual, Maureen stood and waved goodbye at the door as they left. She was the oldest person he had seen in a while. It was the men who were taken away but the women lived on unseen, mouldering in the safety of their own homes. It made him sick to think about it. Which is how he came to promise that they would definitely make for Cornwall before Angela's twenty-first birthday. That was a promise. They would drive slowly and carefully along the back routes. It would take them no more than a day. He had the passes from Jenkins, after all. Their birthdays were around the same time, actually. He would be twenty-five a few days after she turned twenty-one and they would be in Cornwall by then.

At last, they had something to look forward to. Angela was almost dizzy with excitement, staying up late every night when he brought her home from Maureen's so she could select which treasures and keepsakes she would bring with them, having a trial pack then changing her mind, then returning to Maureen's house to chatter to her about it all the next day.

It was a shame Lucas didn't make more of that week. It was the last time he looked forward to anything.

19 Eulogy for Jesmond

Jason Prince was exhausted and emotional, but proud that he'd done the right thing for Jesmond's family. Even though he was so tired, he sat down and worked on the poem he had been trying to write for a few days now, a eulogy that he would have liked to give to Jesmond's family – that extravagantly tired-looking woman, that wan child – wrapped up with the information that it had cost him so much to obtain for them. But he couldn't get the words right and he hadn't wanted to delay their flight while he waited for the muse. Fortunately Jesmond had been fond of the booze, so had some of the rhymes he needed – clink, drink. He had some of the images he wanted – of Jesmond's killers celebrating behind closed doors, dancing and singing, then pausing while one of them held up his hand to say a few words, to acknowledge the eminence of their foe. It wasn't just a mention of the poetry and the songs that had to be worked into the poem, there was the extraordinary act of freeing the animals from the zoos which had made him as famous as anything else he had done. And it needed a killer couple of closing lines. So far he had, '*Jesmond, here's what I believe: you died/ as you lived, because of poetry.*' But did anyone care what Jason believed? Or that the words didn't properly rhyme?

At least he'd been able to enclose the poem about the gauzy veil. It was done on a whim, really, inspired by the woman who lived at the address Jesmond had given him. He hadn't dared put it through the letterbox of that house because of the ministry man. But she must have seen the poem – she spent all day with the woman and child he was now convinced were Jesmond's wife and daughter – and he hoped she'd appreciated it. As friend or kin to a famous poet, she surely would have done.

He wouldn't be able to show this new poem to anyone, for fear of it getting into the wrong hands and making him the target for retribution. He couldn't even say that he hoped Jesmond would see it, wherever he was, because he didn't believe that a person's spirit lived on after he was dead. That's why poetry was so important. Poetry survived.

When he finished it, he would put this piece with the others, and lock them away somewhere, and hope that his work would be found and admired one day after he was gone.

20 Something Closing In

Lucas walked into the Ministry and everything was imperceptibly different. People looked at him oddly. He saw that whatever was to happen next would be beyond his control. It was the same feeling he used to get when it was his turn to be bullied at school. He knew that he could give himself up to it or he could fight, and that how he behaved might affect how people treated him in the future, although it wouldn't affect what was going to happen to him now because it had already been decided.

He thought, am I making this happen or is it happening to me and I'm merely taking note of it? He went and sat in his office and felt frightened. He couldn't say why. Was it the look from the security guard at the front desk as he came in, a taste in the air, a feeling he had? He tried to remember how he'd felt when he'd seen Angela's bloody knickers on the floor, to console himself with a reminder that he had been wrong then.

But he wasn't wrong now. Something was closing in on him. What were his options? What had caused this situation, first of all? If he knew that, then maybe he'd be able to rectify it, to make himself safe.

He had gone to Jones's house and imagined kissing his wife. He had taken pot plants to Maureen's house and received gingerbread in return. He had accepted passes from Jenkins and planned to use them to take Angela to Cornwall. But he hadn't looked at any child pornography or made any bombs. And Jesmond, who had always been there, haunting the periphery of his life, was gone now and couldn't damage him by turning up at his house and tipping off the authorities to their miracle inspector's links to undesirables.

Then it hit him. Maureen. Perhaps Maureen was a terrorist or was known to consort with terrorists. There was no Mr Maureen. Of course, there was always a chance that he had died of natural causes or she had decided to go it alone from the get-go. But perhaps her husband had been considered dangerous and had been taken away by the authorities. Lucas didn't know because you didn't ask. He'd always thought it fortunate that his own father had died of liver failure at the age of thirty-nine, leaving his reputation intact. It was one of the things that had counted in Lucas's favour when he'd been appointed to this job: he had no criminal relatives. His father had actually been highly regarded in some circles, being vaguely aristocratic and monied, and charming when drunk. But without doubt, the thing that had counted for Lucas the most was that his father had never gone to prison. If they'd known that Matthew had written the tunes for those protest songs! But few did – or few in authority, anyway. Jesmond had always been the front man.

Maureen. The more he thought about it, the more it made sense. Of course she was a rebel. An intelligent woman deprived of an interesting job in television news, with a child who didn't receive the level of care she might get elsewhere, in more enlightened states or territories. All that biscuit-making was probably a cover for a home-made bomb factory. Angela spent all day there helping out. There would be spies and surveillance. Everyone would know what she was up to and now the finger would be pointed at him, too. All that crap about taking Christina to the countryside for a picnic. She'd probably been planning to go to a power station and plant a bomb.

Things in his office had been touched. He could see by the way they had been put back a little too neatly. People had looked at him oddly. His wife had been inveigled into bomb-making with a terrorist. He wasn't surprised to look up and see that Jones had wandered into his office. Jones had a little false smile painted into the corners of his mouth from drinking Ribena.

Lucas wondered whether to rush at him shouting 'arghhhhh' and get his hands round Jones's neck; a moment of glory before all Jones's Ribena cronies crowded in from outside and kicked him in the kidneys until he died. Perhaps Jenkins would join forces with him, running in with a bag of cats so they could fling cats at Jones until they were overpowered. He couldn't decide whether Jenkins would be on his side or not. Had he upset Jenkins with all that tosh about the hidden cameras and the pornography or had he helped him to see some higher truth about Jones and himself and the way London was run?

Lucas suddenly saw, with absolute clarity, that Jesmond and his father had been right. It would have been so much better to have been a cheerful, eccentric drunk, pissing off the authorities and being lauded for it by everyone else because he was so entertaining. Why go to work every day, investigating miracles that had never happened, why get up and brush your teeth and make love to your wife and do the washing up when it was all, inevitably, going to end like this, with Jones walking in to his office with a sneer.

But Jones didn't seem to mean him any harm. He was unusually diffident.

'There've been rumours,' he began.

Lucas didn't say anything.

'If you found something, you'd tell me. Wouldn't you, mate?'

Even Jones wanted to believe in miracles. Maybe he should tell Jones he'd gone to his house the other day because Joanna had reported a miracle. It was a brilliant excuse. But Jones might not know anything about the visit, so he'd be taking a risk by mentioning it. If only he could claim immunity before asking certain questions or saying certain things, the way he would if this was all just a game.

'There are proper channels, you know,' Lucas said primly.

'I know,' said Jones. He looked so hopeful, standing there, that Lucas might have warmed to him at last. They might have gone for a beer and talked it over and become friends. But just then, the soldiers came for him.

There were six of them, crowding into the doorway. It would have been impossible to run. Jones looked startled, then frightened, then upset, then helpless. He didn't look as if he was responsible for what was happening, which might have been some comfort to Lucas if the six soldiers had been purely academic and not standing there, panting, stinking, big and real, waving their guns to show that they'd come for him. Lucas saw and understood all of this in the few seconds it took him to locate and fix on Jones's face.

'Help me,' said Lucas. But Jones couldn't.

21 Black Grapes

The light was strange; blueish, damp. Someone with too much time on their hands had scraped the flesh from a bunch of black grapes and stitched the skins together to make a curtain for his eyes.

He felt cold and stiff and dirty, as if he'd spent the night camping in Hyde Park, and he was in pain. He would go to Maureen's house. She'd give him a hot drink and let him have a shower. Angela would be there, looking worried and angry. Her mood would change when she saw what had happened to him. He wouldn't want her to be too nice, in case he started to cry. He'd go and sit next to her and hug her and explain that they had to leave for Cornwall right away. She'd nod towards Maureen, lean in and whisper to him, 'They're coming with us.'

'No,' he'd say. 'I'm sorry.'

Maureen would go to the kitchen and bang some pots fairly loudly, to show she wasn't listening.

'We'd never make it,' he'd say to Angela. 'They'd slow us down.'

Angela would give him that stubborn look, where her face closed in on itself and hardened. It was like watching a clay mask dry on her skin. He'd acquiesce to the demands that they all leave for Cornwall and Maureen would go and pack. And while she was doing that he'd have a shower and wash some of this pain away. When he stepped out of the veil of water in the shower and switched off the tap, it would be like completing the final part of a ceremony, like switching off his connection to this oppressive city. He'd dry himself with one of Maureen's fluffy pink towels and put his fetid clothes back on, or perhaps Maureen would lend him one of her T-shirts. They'd put Maureen's bags into the car, get in, close the doors, get Christina settled, put their seatbelts on. He'd switch the engine on and drive away. They'd leave London forever.

'Mate?' Someone touched his arm, gently. His arms hurt. Blue and bruised, maybe he was the grape, crushed under dozens of stamping toes. They'd make a very sour wine out of him.

'Mate?' Someone wiped a warm, wet flannel over his face, very gently. It was an exquisitely pleasant experience. It was done with maternal kindness. Was he with his mother? He had died and was in the process of being reborn, his poor little body battered by the journey through the birth canal, now delivered to the efficiencies of midwifery to be wiped down tenderly by some maternity nurse. He probably ought to cry out, to show that he was alive.

Someone held a cup of water to his lips. He wondered if he had the strength to go through another life from start to finish. It would be too painful, too full of sorrow and disappointment. He realised he was crying.

Someone began to tell him a story about a man whose shadow had learned to live separately from him. From birthday to story time, his early years seemed to be whizzing by. He didn't remember things going so fast last time round. He didn't want stories, he wanted a lullaby.

Someone knew this. He heard men's voices, deep and low. They were humming. There was something reassuring in the masculinity of the sound. It was a rumble, the distant sound of tanks coming to the rescue through a forest. The sound of angels assembling to fight an evil foe. The tune was lovely, and familiar. When they stopped humming the introduction and started singing the words, he knew why. '*Imagine a land for you and me, without borders or checks on our ID. Imagine no CCTV,*' they sang. '*Rise up.*' That settled it. Jesmond's protest songs would never be heard in heaven. Lucas hadn't died, he hadn't been reborn. He was still alive, left over from last time. It didn't give him any comfort.

22   Waspercise

The next day, or maybe the day after that, Lucas had recovered sufficiently to understand where he was. He watched as a man called Rolf ran up and down the narrow space inside their prison cell, dodging and feinting as if trying to outwit a wasp. He might have been developing a physical training technique. Possibly he was planning to bring out a fitness DVD when he was released. *Rolf Runs with Wasps. Waspercise. Rolfercise.*

Rolf saw Lucas looking and came to sit next to him on the hard bed. Rolf was a very thin man with a bushy black beard. He could have been any age from twenty-five to forty-five and he looked like a desert island companion – not in the sense of being an ideal choice, like when people say for example that their 'desert island' ice cream would be chocolate and cherry, or mango sorbet. Rather, he looked as though he had been living on a desert island for some time. But there was no hushing sound of waves, no coconut trees, no hot sun or salty breeze, no warm sand to wriggle bare toes in, where they were being held.

Lucas wondered why Rolf was wearing someone else's clothes. His shabby trousers were much too big for him and he looked like a scarecrow. Who was he trying to scare? Not Lucas. Lucas didn't care about anything any more. How long had he been there? If someone had said 'forty years' he might have believed them but he supposed it was not that long. He had been there for however long it took for hope to die. How long was that?

'About twenty-four hours,' Rolf said.

'So what's the deal here?' Lucas asked him. He was expecting that Rolf would point out the old-timers, say something about the food.

Instead he said, 'They'll be along in a couple of hours, to take you away for questioning.'

'I'll have a chance to put my case?'

'Naw, you won't get a trial. This is a rubbish tip. They sift through it, trying to harvest anything useful.'

'Like what?'

'Oh,' Rolf laughed. His face showed that he didn't think it was funny. 'Your kidneys are safe, bro. Your gold teeth. They want information.'

'I don't know anything.'

'You'd be surprised. Listen. You got to find a way of leaving yourself behind in there. Yeah? Coercive questioning. It's not very nice. You got to go elsewhere, remember happy times. A day in the park with your mother, when you were small. The smell of your wife's perfume. Or think of a song you like.'

Lucas could think of a song he didn't like. *Rise up, rise up...*

'You got something? Imagine dancing to it. Memorise the steps; the more intricate the better. I imagine this dance, me and my shadow. But while he's dancing, tap tap, tap tap, tap tap, taking it very serious, I leave him here. I'm off. You get me?'

'That's what you were doing just now? Dancing?'

'Practising. We run along, and we're together. I lift my foot, he lifts his. I kick, he kicks. Then, boom, I turn real sharp, wrench my foot away, so I'm out of step with him. And I'm off. I'm outta there.'

'Sounds a bit energetic.'

'It ain't physical, it's philosophical. You gotta get the mental energy right. I'm serious, bro. You need a strategy for when you're in there.'

'I could think about my wife.'

'Alright. So you got yourself something to fix on: her face, her name, the smell of her perfume.'

'You said.'

'That's your portal. Fix on it, orient yourself, then go through. Yeah? Whatever you do, don't just sit in that room staring at the doorway. You gotta get up and go through.'

23 Woo!

The interrogator was a young man. He had a likeable face and spiky 'woo, I'm a little bit crazy' hair, like an enthusiastic art master at one of those progressive schools that probably still existed outside London. He gave the impression that he and Lucas were in this thing together, and that while he might know more than Lucas about the situation they found themselves in – had, in fact, been here many times before – he wasn't going to patronise Lucas by making it obvious. He was actually going to pretend that they were setting off on a journey of discovery together and that they'd both find it equally instructional and equally entertaining.

The interrogator couldn't sit still. He got up, paced about. He was so animated, so eager, Lucas felt he would have been more suited to the role of children's entertainer and had surely only fallen into the interrogation business because so few opportunities came up in children's entertainment these days. In fact, if they were on the outside – where, as a government employee, Lucas had had a little influence – he might have tried to make a few enquiries, see if he could do something for the poor bloke. He wasn't sure if he had caught his name, was it Terry? Terry Gator would be an excellent stage name. But they weren't on the outside. They were on the inside, where their situations were reversed and the bloke had all the influence and Lucas had none at all.

'Your wife,' said the interrogator. 'Had she been planning a trip somewhere?'

Lucas remembered what Rolf had said. That was the portal. He tried to think about Angela and what she was doing now. He imagined her sitting at home, grief-stricken, her face red and blotchy from crying, which always made her look as if she had been stung all over by nettles. She was sitting in the kitchen. She looked listless, more depressed than he had ever seen her. Someone was with her. Who was it? Delilah? Joanna Jones? Maureen, standing about, looking embarrassed? Perhaps they were all there, trying to cheer her up while silently disapproving of him.

No, that wouldn't do at all. He didn't want to think of Angela sitting at home waiting for him. He wanted to imagine her on her way to Cornwall. When he didn't come to collect her from Maureen's, Angela would know he must be in trouble. An hour would go by, then another. She'd begin to make plans to flee.

24 Going Underground

Angela went to the bathroom and vomited in the toilet, the shameful smell creeping out through the house and giving her away. Maureen said nothing. If they were going to go on the road together, there would be many more instances when they would be aware of each others' bodies and their weaknesses.

'Perhaps they're holding him for questioning and they'll release him?' Angela said to Maureen.

'Yes. I hope so.'

Presumably Lucas's car was at the Ministry. But even if he had conveniently left it parked outside Maureen's house and decided to walk into work or cycle there for some reason, it would have been no use to the women. Neither of them could drive. Their best hope for a way out of London was the message that had come through Maureen's door from 'a well-wisher'.

It turned out that 'Go down to Down Street' was not an especially cryptic message. Maureen looked in her encyclopaedia. Down Street was an underground station with its entrance on Down Street, just off Piccadilly. It had briefly served as a bunker for the Cabinet Office in the last war, in 1939, but it had been abandoned as a railway station in 1932, long, long before the whole underground system had fallen into disuse, the stations boarded up, the lifts disconnected and the stairs smashed to prevent people living down there.

'Perhaps we should wait twenty-four hours?' Angela said. 'In case he comes back. He might have been held up at work. He might have found a miracle.' She picked up the phone in Maureen's house to check there was a dialling tone. It was working OK. She phoned her home but there was no answer. Lucas hadn't gone back there. She phoned his office but she got a recorded message. *'If you are calling to report a miracle, press 1 now. If you are calling to check on the status of a report you have already made, press 2.'* She put the phone down.

'There's only one reason a man doesn't come home from work at night,' Maureen said. 'Well, two reasons. But you'd have heard from him by now if it was the second.'

'Maybe I should go to the Ministry?'

'You could,' said Maureen. 'It's up to you. Is there anyone you trust who you can call?'

But there wasn't.

After two hours, Maureen packed a bag with clothes and provisions. After three, she turned the gas off at the wall. She turned off the water. She unplugged all the appliances, closed the curtains.

'Perhaps we ought to wait?' Angela said.

'Could do. How long have you been waiting for your dad to come back?'

'Nine years.'

They left the house with Christina and two small bags. Angela would have to wear Maureen's clothes until they got to Cornwall. She couldn't risk a return home in case the house was being watched. It would not have been wise to have been seen leaving home with a suitcase so soon after her husband's disappearance.

They got to Piccadilly before the curfew, walking part of the way behind a shepherd herding his sheep from Green Park to graze them in Hyde Park. London was quiet and peaceful – it almost seemed a shame to leave. In Down Street they found the lovely red-tiled facade of the abandoned Tube station just to the side of a newsagent's shop. There was no padlock on the door. They opened it and saw the spiral staircase that would take them down into the system of tunnels beneath them; it was still intact. They started to walk down it into the darkness, Maureen in front, Angela behind, Christina in between them.

'This seems quite straightforward,' said Angela, apparently heedless of how much she was likely to antagonise the gods with such a remark. There was a sharp, damp smell in the air, cobwebs hung on the stair rail, and the paint was peeling off the walls. As they descended, the air grew warmer. Below them she heard eerie shrieks and caught a whiff of the distinctive odour of urine.

'There's something down here,' Angela said. 'Something moving, reaching out from the walls.'

169

'An enchanted forest? You're not used to the dark, that's all. It's what comes of respecting the curfew.'

As they reached the bottom of the stairway, Angela could feel the empty flapping of Maureen's hand as she felt for Christina's hand. But the child slipped past her mother and kept walking. How had they ever thought this would work?

'Christina!' called Maureen, her voice so rich with feeling, it was like hearing a whole opera in one word. Christina turned back and put her hand in her mother's hand.

Angela found a torch in her rucksack and shone it the length of the corridor. There was only a door behind a metal grille and a strange, other-worldly blue glow coming from behind the door. As they got near, the door opened to reveal a large, bright, cheery room decorated with funky patterned wallpaper, 1970s plastic bucket chairs on stalks, beaded standard lamps and an aquarium. The place smelled of coffee. Plinky bossa nova cocktail music was playing. It was empty except for a young woman in an aquamarine cat suit.

'Hi,' she said, 'I'm Tawny. Did you bring the toll?'

'What do you need?' Maureen asked. 'If we've got it, we'll be happy to share it with you.'

'Aloe vera,' said Tawny. 'Plants, sunshine, fish, parsley, paperback books, fuses.'

They had neither fish nor fuses, nor any of the other things Tawny had asked for, as Maureen very well knew. Still, she searched through the contents of her rucksack with great solemnity, as if she really thought she might find some sunshine in there. Eventually she came up with a jar of multi-vitamins, some soluble Vitamin C tablets and some gingerbread, which she handed over.

The eerie wails started up again. 'Sensors,' said Tawny. 'It's on a loop. You get used to it.'

'How did you get the screaming noises?' Angela asked her.

'Foxes. And what about the hands coming out of the walls? Neat idea, isn't it? We take it in turns.'

'I thought I felt something!'

'Jezza's down there now. Squeeze your tits, did he? Cheeky bugger. We want some automata – there's some at the Clink Museum or the London Dungeon we could filch, if the other trolls haven't had them already. Getting them across London's too hazardous – underground, OK, no trouble. But we'd have to bring them some of the way over ground.'

'Automata?' said Angela.

There was a clanking sound as three or four sure-footed men came down the spiral staircase.

'Sound as if they know their way here,' said Tawny. 'Smugglers, probably. Let's hope they've brought my parsley. Best get you hid. They're dangerous.'

'Parsley smugglers?'

'People smugglers. Cash up front, don't take kindly to rivals on their turf. Know what I mean?'

Tawny took them towards the source of the blue light. She saw the puzzled look on Angela's face and said, 'Guess what it is.'

A giant electric fly killer? A tub of radium? A time machine? A device which might summon Jesmond here to tell Angela what was in the rest of the letters he'd written twenty years before? A device which might allow her to go back just two or three weeks to warn Lucas not to do whatever it was that had got him taken away. If only she knew. If only he knew.

'It's a solarium,' said Tawny. 'I'm gonna do you a favour, for the sake of the kid. Wait in there till those blokes have gone by then head west down the tunnels towards Heathrow. Get out at Terminal Five.'

'Do the planes still fly?' asked Angela. 'We were thinking of going to Australia.'

Tawny turned to Maureen. 'There's a break in the perimeter fence by Terminal Five. Squeeze through, it brings you up outside the London borders. Don't hang about because when they find it, they'll repair it.'

'Thanks,' said Maureen.

'Don't you ever think of going?' asked Angela.

'This is me. This is what I do. There's absolutely no guarantee there's anything better out there. You go if you want, I'm not stopping you. The fences won't stay up forever. I'll see what I want to do then.'

'I expect you're right,' said Maureen. 'But we can't wait.'

'Make sure you claim asylum as soon as you get to Slough or you'll find yourselves back here.' Tawny said. She gave Angela a compass. 'I got it off a dead man. Hope it does you more good than it did him.'

25 An Awful Sour Smell

'Mate?' There was an awful sour smell. Lucas couldn't think what it was, where he was. Then he remembered and he waited a moment or two before opening his eyes. He had soiled himself, or Rolf had. He didn't want to see it or engage with it or help clear it up.

'Mate? Come on. Please.' Rolf's voice, wheedling. A hand on his arm. He opened his eyes, saw that the stink came from a bowl of brown liquid next to his bed, a modest-sized turd floating in it.

Lucas knew all about the symptoms of distress shown by caged animals in zoos – standing and rocking or nodding their heads repeatedly, and eating their own faeces. Jesmond used to go on and on about it before freeing as many of them as he could from London Zoo in Regent's Park and going on the run. So when Rolf dipped a spoon into the bowl of filth and brought it to his lips, Lucas wasn't as shocked as another man might have been. He took hold of Rolf's arm very gently and said, 'No.'

'You got to have nourishment,' said Rolf. 'It's all there is.'

Then Lucas saw that the brown liquid was a soup of some kind. The fibrous, fatty chunk floating in it was not a turd but had once been alive, though whether animal or vegetable he still wasn't sure. Life in prison was almost comically unpleasant, a child's version of what a prison should be, unbendingly awful and without comfort or humanity of any kind. It was an environment created by people without imagination or wit. The big question was, why?

'Think you might have found a miracle and not known it?' Rolf asked.

'You're joking. People called up, hoping it would lead to something, that I'd pull some strings, that I'd write them a note to see a doctor, or ask someone to pop by and sort out their garden, or their cooker or their drains. It never happened but they never stopped hoping. Got depressing, after a while, especially when you realise they'd be glad of a visit from just about any Ministry department inspecting just about anything: cats, rapists, miracles, whatever.'

'Something happened that's got you in here, bro.'

There had been a number of cats touted by their owners as having a special skill. His favourite among these had been the clairvoyant tabby cross. There had been wise, clever, talented children, many of whom had been able to play the piano to a high standard at an early age. He had sat through a lot of recitals. He had inspected spiders and dandelion heads mistaken for angels, feathers and gnats mistaken for fairies, and religious iconography

174

that had spontaneously appeared in baked goods all over London. He had declared none of them a miracle.

'Must have been nice to spend time with the kids? One of the few men allowed within five feet of a child without his wife having given birth to it. And even then...'

'You've got to have precautions. You don't want to end up like the French or the Spanish – strangers hugging and kissing babies, grandparents allowed to help care for the kids.'

'That's a myth,' Rolf said.

Even if Rolf had relatives in one of those countries, it was near impossible that he'd been in touch with any of them at any time in the last twenty years to verify what life was like there. Still, Lucas was conciliatory. 'They don't touch kids, you mean?'

'Playing with kids doesn't make you a paedophile, is what I mean.'

A clue as to what Rolf was in there for? Perhaps it was as well to stick with an analysis of why Lucas might have been taken. Where were they?

Rolf said, 'You were talking about miracles.'

Poltergeists and ghosts were popular, particularly in north London. Ethereal singing was heard more often in South London than in any other quarter. People made urgent, desperate phone calls to his office: a spirit had a message it wished to convey to 'the cynics'; it could help, it could heal, it had foretold the end of the world or the beginning of a new era. It could lead the authorities to where the body of the last Queen of England lay. But

Lucas never heard anything more remarkable than bird song when he visited these hauntings, leaving him no choice but to report, as ever, that a miracle had not been found.

He had also been asked to inspect several inventions. Ordinary people had very little access to information so they couldn't readily discover whether the 'miraculous' labour-saving devices they came up with had already been invented. Some of the inventions were daft and some showed ingenuity. Many of the inventors had been motivated by an altruism that had given Lucas a quiet hope for the future. In every case, he had followed the correct procedure and passed details of the reported invention to the person at the Ministry who was responsible for inspecting them.

When he was first appointed to the role of miracle inspector, he had assumed that there would be weeks or months on end without news of a miracle. But he was called out almost daily. Some of the people who contacted him were in earnest, some mischievous, some pathetic. The worst of them were his 'regulars', who would contact him time and again, as if sooner or later he must give in and start handing out prizes for effort.

'The last visit, mate? Might be something in that.'

The last visit he'd made had been to Christina; very thin and frail, she had looked about five years old. Perhaps she was older. It hardly mattered: in the reporting of miracles, appearances trumped facts, always.

'Any chance she was the real deal?'

'No. Sweet kid but she couldn't talk. She just lay there. I couldn't see her saving a life or… You know. My wife liked her.'

'You let your wife out of the house?'

'No one knew. She wanted to go and sing to the child. We couldn't… We didn't have one of our own. It was only once. No one saw us.'

Rolf shook his head, weary and wise. But thinking about his job had been restorative for Lucas. It had connected him to his old self, the inspector, the man from the Ministry. It was the next best thing to clothing him in a suit and sending him back out into the world.

He felt he had got a hold of himself. Then he was called in for interrogation again.

26 The Serpent and the Singing

'Lucas?' Someone was whispering, shaking him. 'Lucas, Lucas?' A man's voice, hissing. He was surprised that he had never noticed the sibilant snake sound that could be made by drawing out the s at the end of his name. It was the wheedling, hissy sound the serpent must have made in paradise.

He was not in paradise. He opened his eyes and looked. He was astonished to see Jesmond standing there, looking very dishevelled. As he looked, he thought he had found an explanation for the hissing sound because it seemed that a dozen snakes had wound themselves around Jesmond and were crawling about his midriff, so many of them that they were having trouble clinging to him and were spilling out of his shirt. Then he saw that the snakes were not snakes but Jesmond's guts. He had been partially disembowelled, the tubes of his innards falling out of his shirt.

As if embarrassed at presenting himself so poorly, Jesmond tried to tuck himself in. He put his shoulders back, stood a little straighter, wiped a hand over his hair and down the length of his curls, to his collar. He shouldn't have done that. Now he had blood on his hair. It might have some nutritional value (didn't people put beer on their hair, blood and bones on their gardens?) but it would dry stiffly, and Jesmond would be sorry about that.

Lucas would have liked to say something, to tip him off about the blood on his hair, but washing facilities were limited so Jesmond couldn't very well rectify it if he wanted to. And anyway, he had closed his eyes and started to croon. He swayed slightly on his feet. The moonlight fell from the window of Lucas's cell onto the white shirt Jesmond was wearing. With the help of the romantic lighting conditions, Lucas now saw how the curls of Jesmond's intestines complemented the curls of his grey hair, as if it had been his intention all along to co-ordinate his appearance by slitting open his belly and teasing out the tubes and arranging them there, fluffing and fussing until he had transformed his appearance, avoiding a potentially unmodish 'unspooled cassette tape' style by going for the much smarter 'gift-wrapped' look. Lucas had seen women (well, Angela) draw the sharp blade of a pair of scissors along the length of a piece of gift-wrapping ribbon to make it curl. The effect that Jesmond had achieved with his intestines was not dissimilar, but it was certainly more masculine. A man might look butch and brave in a skirt, if he calls it a kilt and knows how to wear it. And that was what Jesmond had done with the potentially frivolous gift-wrap effect of his intestines. He'd made it look butch. He was to be commended.

For a moment, Lucas felt intensely happy. Then he felt desolate. Then it didn't matter what he felt because Jesmond tried to take over his mood and steer it somewhere else by singing to him.

'You know I've loved you all your life?' sang Jesmond. *'Hmmm, yeah.'*

'Yeah, I know,' sang Lucas (somewhat to his own surprise). *'You're my godfather, right? I guess I knew you'd show up here one night.'*

'The disembowelment doesn't bother you? I didn't give you a fright?'

'It's not too bad — it looks quite nice, the way your intestines glisten in the moonlight, mmm.'

'Mmmmm, right. There's something else you need to know, hmmm.'

'Is it Angela? Is she alright? Hmmm. Can you tell me, can you tell me, can you tell me, yeah?'

'Lucas, I don't know, woah, oh. I guess she's on her way to Cornwall but I didn't see her go. No. Mmmm. Yeah.'

'Oh? O-oh. Hmmm. What did you come to tell me then, is it something bad?'

'No, Lucas, no. Oh-o. I've come to let you know… that I'm your Dad.'

'Chri-i-i-i-i-i-st. Woah-oh. Wooo-oo-ooh.'

'I thought you might have guessed?'

'That you'd slept with my mum? No. I never knew-ooh-oh. I never knew, hmm.'

'Son, you know I always loved you? I loved your mum, too.'

'Jesmond, I don't care. Get out of here. And, Jesmond?

'Yes?'

'I lied about your intestines; they look a mess.'

And then as he watched, Jesmond seemed to fade away, 'mmmming' and 'oh yeah-ing' as he went. Finally, there was no trace of him except a low rumbling sound.

Lucas tried to think of something else, something nicer. He thought about Angela, on her way to Cornwall; to safety.

27 Slough

As soon as they slipped through the fence into Slough, they were picked up by border guards who gave them two choices – claim asylum or face deportation back to London. There was no 'just passing through' option. They claimed asylum and were handed over to a woman named Fenella at the Refugee Centre.

'You must be hungry,' said Fenella. 'Let's get something to eat. Is Tina hungry?'

'Christina.'

'Are you hungry, dear? What does she like to eat, Maureen? We've no jellied eels, I'm afraid, though there's a lovely little Cockney Shop across the other side of town. I must take you to it one day. The pie and mash is lovely. That green stuff, what's it called?'

In Slough, Maureen and Angela looked out of place. Maureen was wearing a shirt-waisted dress and Angela was wearing a pair of trousers and a shirt that belonged to Maureen. Their clothes were not awful but when the women of Slough swished by, insouciant and stylish in flattering clothes, the patterns and fabrics they wore referenced each other as if they were part of some

182

fabulous exhibition that had been curated by a *professor* of fashion. Any half a dozen Slough women, taken at random from the streets and arranged on white boxes in a white room, would have looked as if they belonged together, some part of a greater whole. Maureen and Angela did not. They did not fit in. They stood there, Christina between them, their luggage in their outer hands, Christina's hands in the hands that hung between them, and they worried about what was going to happen next.

'Fugees,' two teenagers said, sneering as they went past.

Angela didn't know how they knew. She and Maureen weren't wearing their covers. They were trying to blend in.

'Take no notice. Come on, we'll go to my house.'

Maureen said, 'You're sure it's no trouble, Fenella? We weren't expecting anything like this.'

'It's no trouble at all. It's good for my kids to see how the other half lives.'

Angela thought about Jesmond. She wondered how he would write about such a place in one of his letters. Then she wondered how she would describe the place to Lucas, if she ever got the chance. He'd always known more about everything than she had, travelled further and met more people. Now she was the explorer. It was a renegotiation of the terms of their relationship.

Over dinner, Fenella introduced them to Tom, her husband.

'He's a playwright,' she said. She left a pause after she'd said it, as if she was expecting them to applaud.

'Verbatim theatre,' Tom said, with a self-deprecating smile, as if they might know what that conjunction of words meant, and therefore would understand that it was something so important and clever that he was embarrassed to mention it because it seemed boastful. But neither Angela nor Maureen had ever been to the theatre. Theatre was banned in London because it was thought to be inflammatory.

'Your husband?' Tom said to Angela. 'He spoke out against the regime, did he?'

'There's not usually a reason why. They just get taken.'

'But he was an artist of some sort? A poet?'

'He was a miracle inspector,' Angela said.

'Oh,' said Fenella.

'He believed in miracles?' asked Tom.

'Tom,' said Fenella. He was too far away to be kicked under the table so she tried to do it with her smile, which was very bright and as curved and stiff as the hook on a coat hanger. If she'd been able to peel it off her face, she could have poked him with it.

Angela saw what Tom wanted. 'Actually, he did speak out. It was heroic, what he did.'

Tom raised his glass to Angela and nodded. 'I'm working on something called *Testimony of a Widow*,' he said. 'Perhaps we could talk about your situation, later.'

'I'm hoping Lucas is still alive,' Angela said.

'Yes, yes, yes,' said Fenella. 'Tom, you could do a piece called *The Miracle Inspector* – that's a nice title.'

'Yes,' said Tom. 'It is.'

'Won't you eat your meal?' asked Fenella.

'Sorry,' said Angela. 'We're not used to meat.'

'There are people in Slough who'd be glad of what you've left on your plates,' said Fenella.

'Leave them alone,' said Tom. 'It's only the wealthy who can afford the bribes to get out of London. I don't expect they're used to our gristly fare.'

Maureen smiled politely, making no effort to finish the food. But Angela felt guilty. She tried to feed herself and Christina. Christina began to choke on a piece of food. Maureen jumped up and banged Christina on the back. Angela couldn't help it. She began to cry.

28 Moon Man

The man who was interviewing Lucas today had slack, grey skin and dark patches under his eyes. He looked as if he was made of moon dust. Not the bright and beautiful fairytale kind that might make him look as if he had been carved from a block of marble like a Rodin sculpture. It was more prosaic than that, closer to real life. The man looked as though he had been moulded from crumbly, volcanic rock that would dirty your hands when you touched him. Lucas felt he could have drawn a hand across the man's face and used the grey ash he collected on his fingertips to write HELP! on the wall behind him. But who would come?

'There's only a few of us here,' Lucas said. 'Is this a prison for the elite?'

'Is that what you think?'

'Is it?'

'Perhaps it is.'

The interrogator had a small bag in front of him, somewhere in size between a pencil case and the sort of fancy wash bag Lucas might have taken on holiday to an expensive hotel, if he had ever been on holiday. The interrogator began to open it.

'You and your wife were planning on going away somewhere?' the interrogator enquired. It was a hairdresser's question. Lucas half expected the man to produce a comb and one of those pairs of silver scissors with a specially-moulded thumb grip from the bag, and give him a quick trim to smarten him up before the trip.

But he didn't.

Lucas tried to think of something that would take him away. The portal. The door. The door or the portal, which was it? Never mind, he had to think of Angela.

29 Anal

By the time dinner was over, Fenella seemed to have grown quite fond of them. 'I'm sorry to have to turn you over to Natalia,' she said, with tears in her eyes. 'I'm sure you'll like her – everybody does. She's got that wonderful Cockney sense of humour.'

'How much do we owe you?' said Maureen, opening her handbag.

'Your currency's no good here. Worthless. It's the trade restrictions. Don't worry about it. Natalia's going to help you to integrate and show you how you can make a living here. It's all funded by the taxpayer. You can stay as long as you like.'

'We're not planning on staying,' Angela said.

Maureen said, 'It's not that we don't like Slough.'

'Don't tell me – you're heading for Cornwall. What is it with Cornwall? Everyone thinks it's beaches, ice cream, walks along the cliffs, fresh fish. You do realise the place has terrible social problems? There's very low employment. What you gonna do? Get a job collecting seaweed? You're much better off here. When your papers come through, you can get a job in Eye Tee.'

Angela would have loved a job in a tea shop, a little frilly pinny, a pad to write the orders on, cucumber sandwiches served with the crusts cut off and home-made cakes or jam and scones. She'd seen it in the films on TV. It was so old-fashioned, it was something Jesmond might have written a poem about.

'No,' said Fenella. 'Not High Tea. Eye Tee. Computers. Mind, it's very well-paid.'

Angela wanted to like Natalia but she found it tough going from the moment she opened her door to them and said, 'Welcome to the Fugee Farm.'

She showed them their room upstairs and then took them into the sitting room where she handed Christina the most extraordinary toy Angela had ever seen; it was a small-scale slut. 'A Bratz doll,' explained Natalia. 'They're all the rage here.'

'It looks just like you,' said Angela. But she was keen to throw off the conditioning of her upbringing and if a close appreciation of their host's bosoms, bottom and thighs jiggling under clingy, revealing clothes was going to help set Angela free, so be it.

Natalia did her best to make them comfortable. First, she poured wine for Angela and Maureen. Next, she painted their fingernails and toenails with expensive varnish which she said was the latest fashion and very difficult to get hold of.

'The dark chocolate cherry colour will mark you out as ladies with attitude and style,' she said firmly. 'And it's long-lasting.'

'Ladies!' said Angela.

'Where we come from,' said Maureen, 'you're a girl until you're eighteen, and after that you're a woman – unless you sell yourself for money, in which case you're a lady.'

'Don't forget,' said Natalia, warming the bottle of nail varnish by rubbing it briskly between the palms of her hands, 'I came from there too.' She grabbed hold of Angela's right hand and pressed it flat on the table, then she opened the nail varnish by gripping the plastic top securely between her teeth while twisting the glass bottle anti-clockwise with her right hand.

Angela didn't really want to have her nails painted. But now that she was emancipated, everyone she met seemed to insist that she do something she didn't want to do.

'C'mere, darling,' Natalia said to Christina after she had finished with Maureen and Angela, drawing the child towards her. 'Come and have some varnish on yer fingers and toes.'

'No,' said Maureen. 'Not for Christina.'

'It's alright,' said Natalia. 'I don't mind.' She held the child's wrists in turn, loosely, and drew the brush from cuticle to tip ten times.

'Tell you what,' Natalia said once the varnish had dried, while they were having another glass of wine and Christina was playing with her unsuitable toy, 'come and have a look at this.'

She took them to a computer screen that had been set up on a side table and switched on the machine. They'd had a lesson in how to integrate, and now Angela assumed they were about to get a demonstration of how to earn a living in Slough, possibly by getting a job in Eye Tee. But when the screen came to life, Natalia showed them page after page of photos of men and women touting themselves in an online brothel.

Natalia brought up a photo of herself on screen. She said, 'Come and see what I've said about me. It's s'posed to be what yer mates would say if they had to describe you to a fella. You read it fer us, Ange.'

'She likes long walks in the rain.'

'You got to have one sporty element,' said Natalia.

'She loves red wine, oranges, sunshine and elephants. Her favourite food is lasagne. She's got a great sense of humour. She's thoughtful and kind. She enjoys shopping for handbags and shoes – but watch out, fellas! When it comes to fashion, she can be bit anal.'
Angela shuddered at this. *'She's an independant lady–'*

'I think you need an e for independent,' Maureen said.

'Maureen used to be a journalist,' said Angela. But Natalia looked wary and slightly upset.

'Actually I noticed a few men on there who said they were looking for an independant woman,' said Maureen. 'Perhaps a is better.'

Angela continued reading: *'She's an independant lady who needs a cuddle sometimes – and she likes to give cuddles, too. Will you take a chance and let her be your cuddle dispenser?'*

'Well,' Natalia asked. 'What d'yer think?'

30 First Impression

Angela lay next to Maureen in bed. Christina was on a blow-up mattress on the floor beside them. It was about 2 o'clock in the morning and, after a few hours of deep, drunken sleep, Angela was awake and feeling troubled. She was dehydrated, cold and shivery. Her heart was beating slightly faster than normal, a hurried, shallow flutter in her chest. Her head ached. She was piecing things together in her mind.

'I'm sorry to have to turn you over to Natalia,' Fenella had said, tears in her eyes. 'She'll show you how to make a living here.' Natalia had called this place a Fugee Farm. What was she farming, exactly?

Angela examined the evidence; the sexual doll and what Natalia called a 'dating site', which she had at first assumed to be an online brothel. What if her first impression had been the correct one? Angela knew what was going on, she'd heard about it often enough in London, although she'd always thought the reports were silly scare stories, promulgated to keep women afraid and locked inside their homes: they were being groomed.

She got up, woke Maureen and tried to wake Christina as quietly as possible, so as not to disturb their host. Maureen lay there, perplexed, taking a bit too long to come to.

'We have to leave,' said Angela, hurriedly packing their things into their bags. She didn't even stop to use the loo.

It wasn't until they had walked for at least half a mile that Angela explained her fears that they were being groomed as sex workers, their services to be advertised online on the site Natalia had shown them that evening. Maureen didn't scold her or try to reassure her. She nodded a few times and they kept walking. They had burnt their bridges, after all.

They travelled west across the city. When they got to the 'Welcome to Slough' sign (there was no 'goodbye' sign, perhaps its inhabitants thought no one would ever want to leave), Angela squatted and peed. Even if the sign makers of Slough didn't think that anyone would ever leave, the fence makers knew better. They had constructed a seven-foot-tall metal turnstile out of horizontal, spiked bars spaced about six inches apart, which turned one way only, allowing users to egress. Maureen, Angela and Christina egressed.

31 The Shadow

Lucas was thinking about his mother. He was probably not the only man in prison thinking about his mother, although the other men were presumably thinking about their own mothers, not about Anna Gray.

His father had given him a locket decorated with pearls and chips of rubies, which had once belonged to her. It had a photo of Lucas aged about three or four years old in it, and the design was very feminine, so he'd had no use for it – who wears a photo of himself around his neck? He had given it to Angela when they married.

His mother had been big on choices. You follow a certain path, the choice you make dictates what happens to you. She didn't like the notion that everything is preordained and it doesn't matter much what you do because you'll reach the same goal in the end. She had accepted, of course, that we all die in the end – all except the disappeared. He was one of them now.

He wondered if his mother could have got to Cornwall. Hadn't his father told him she had run away?

'She was painting portals into other worlds? That's so cool,' said Rolf when Lucas told him about Anna.

'It was an art project, that's all. She had a good imagination.'

'You thought of using it, in there?'

'I don't know if I can remember any of the pictures clearly enough.'

'Concentrate, it'll come back to you. Gather all the things you remember about her in one place in your mind, like making a shrine. It'll help.'

'Is that what you do?'

'No. I told you. I go in with my shadow. Then when they start in, I get up, quick as I can, whoosh, and leave him behind.'

'Where do you go? Outside?'

'Yeah.'

'You fly?'

'Yeah. But not the whooshing, swooping kind you get when you dream about flying. Not even the leg-kicking, splashing, swimming kind. I feel the outside air on my skin and I mingle with it, like smoke drifting up above a chimney towards the clouds. It's not mechanical. It's transcendental, I'm hardly aware of it. I'm like... I'm aware I've done it, after.'

'What if you travel too far away and leave him behind? That's got to be risky.'

'Risk, risk, risk, risk, risk, risk, risk.' Rolf was so het up he was making a sound like a flustered hostess at a dinner party, grating a nearly-overlooked nutmeg just in time to garnish the spinach mousse. 'You're so concerned with risk. How did you ever get put in here?'

Lucas stared at his friend. Rolf was thinner than ever. The skin that stretched over his skull was dry and delicate, as if he was dead already and his shadow had climbed inside the cadaver and was wearing him like a monkey suit.

Lucas said, 'Doesn't he get resentful, being left behind?'

'They don't feel pain like we do.'

'Have you ever come face to face with each other? Would you even recognise him?'

Rolf rallied a bit. 'Imagine a sepia photo of a man printed on baking paper, crunched up and put in a pocket. Yeah? Maybe the picture shows him walking towards you, or it's a face, or a shoulder and the back of the head as he runs away. Anyways, it's a figure in motion, an image taken at random. Most likely it's blurred. Take the piece of paper from your pocket, smooth out the creases, look at it. Close up it's a page of faded dots of a similar colour: disparate, yeah? Meaningless. But hold it further away, it starts to look like a man. I know him, bro, even when he's separate from me.'

'Sounds like one of the miracles I used to investigate.'

'Nah. We've all got a shadow. Though who's to say if you're born with one or if they're little dark demons that attach to you when you come out into the world, and they grow with you. You know? It's a way for them to live, yeah? They go where you go.'

'In which case ours won't be very happy, being in here.'

'You're not kidding.'

'Ever worry yours might try and escape? Leave you in here. If you can separate, it must work both ways.'

'I'm working on a strategy to address that. I been perfecting a technique of sharing energy. He grows more substantial, I become slighter. He gets a better chance of surviving without me, I get a better chance to escape.'

'Well, look at you. It seems to be working.'

'You wanna try?'

'I don't think it'll work if I don't believe in it. Sorry.'

'Nah, that's OK.'

'You discussed it with anyone else in here?'

'Not many. They don't stay long.'

'Where do they go, after here?'

Rolf took a while to respond. It seemed he was trying to work out whether Lucas already knew the answer. 'Maybe they go somewhere better,' he said eventually.

Lucas would never know whether his friend had managed to drain away just enough of himself to separate permanently from his shadow, slip out through the bars and fly away free. After that night, he never saw Rolf – or his shadow – again.

32 The Custard Slice

Angela, Maureen and Christina had been walking steadily for days now, averaging ten to fifteen miles a day, keeping to the back roads and the quiet country lanes through Berkshire and Wiltshire. Sometimes they were silent. Sometimes Angela sang. Their feet ached. At night they slept all curled up together in the hedgerows, with their two bags as pillows for their three heads, and Maureen's clothes piled on top of them for warmth. Then when daylight came, they set off again, taking it in turns to carry Christina, or letting her walk.

Whenever they heard the sound of a vehicle approaching, they ducked behind the nearest hedge or a tree and kept out of sight. Usually the vehicle was a big white jeep used by one of the innumerable NGOs and UN Peacekeepers who had shown up after partition, billeted themselves in the grand country house hotels in the most troubled regions, and made it their remit to make recommendations to various committees about how to improve the lives of the local people.

The jeeps were usually going very fast, the occupants accelerating as they approached the bends in the road, hooting their horns almost continually to warn oncoming vehicles to get out of the way. Fortunately, they were too taken up with their own masterful self-importance to look out of the window, notice the walking party hiding in the hedge, and interfere with their progress.

Sometimes Angela and Maureen stopped at a farm and asked to buy a glass of milk for Christina. People were kind. They seemed to have very little money – a large slice of what they earned was levied to pay for the UN presence – but they almost always gave Maureen or Angela a cup of coffee or tea when they called at the door, or a paper bag with half a dozen hard-boiled eggs in it, or a slice of apple pie for the journey. They'd give a glass of milk and some chocolate or an apple to Christina, refusing to take payment for any of it – even sometimes giving them a few coins to buy provisions at the next village. 'We know what it means to be poor,' they'd say. 'Good luck to you.'

They got to the outskirts of a village in Somerset and it was sunny, so they went into a field and lay on the grass in the sun. There were buttercups and cowslips in the field. Birds were singing. A river ran by. Angela took in all of it, considered it, appreciated it. She was truly happy. She sang a few bars of 'Summertime' and Maureen lay back on the grass with her eyes closed and listened, and when Angela had finished, she applauded, bringing her hands together about five times, quite slowly and heavily, to make a dry clapping sound. 'Lovely,' she said. 'Really lovely.'

Angela looked over at Christina, lying on the grass. She looked at Maureen. Maureen opened her eyes, made the peak of a cap with the curve of her hand, keeping the sun out of her eyes so she could look at Angela. She smiled.

Angela loved Maureen as a mother, sister, friend, lover – it defied categorisation. She wondered why men and women got married. It was nice to have a man for sex, especially in the early days, and they were still needed for the practicalities of creating children. But women made much better companions. She could imagine living with Maureen and being happy with her for the rest of her life.

Maureen sat up and began talking about Christina and her hopes for the child; that something – some outside stimulus or attendance at school, or the provision of medicine – would unlock her world for her. She talked about her father, a brilliant man and the author of such scientific studies as *Given the Time Taken to Load the Dishwasher, Wouldn't it be Quicker Just to Wash the Dishes Ourselves?* He had invented a cost-effective, ecological fuel alternative to oil called Maureenozene. But because of vested interests from fuel companies (he'd said) it had not been taken up worldwide. He had encouraged his daughter to study and make her way in the world. She had been bright, able, with a keen sense of justice and had managed to get herself taken on as a trainee reporter with a local TV station when she was only 17 years old. Her father had been one of the early disappeared. Before he was taken, he had transferred to his daughter all the money he had earned from his inventions, and this she carried with her now in a bag in stacks of notes in large denominations – his life savings. Useless anywhere except London.

'I wonder at what point we have to accept that they're never coming back? I mean, I suppose your dad would be dead by now anyway,' Angela said. She was thinking aloud, really, thinking about her own father.

'He'd only be seventy-seven,' said Maureen. 'How old do you think I am?'

They walked up the path into the village to buy a few provisions with some coins they had been given at one of the farms. It was such a peaceful, pretty village, Angela wondered whether they might settle here and find work. Why keep going, inviting trouble by crossing more borders?

While Maureen went to buy, apples, cheese and tomatoes, Angela waited with their bags, looking at the display in the bakery window with Christina. There were pink iced pigs and white mice for sale, birthday cakes with greetings inked on them in chocolate-coloured letters, slabs of strawberry cake, buns, meat pies and sausage rolls. Christina seemed to be particularly interested in the custard slices. Angela joined the queue in the bakery, paid for a loaf of bread – she chose a large bloomer, because of the name. Then, on the way out – it was such a silly thing to do – as they passed the window display, she reached out and snatched a custard slice, and carried on walking. She didn't think anyone would notice.

'Hey!'

She didn't even have to turn around. She knew. She'd blown it. It was a man's voice, rough, aggressive.

'Hey!' he said again. 'Hey! She took that cake.'

A few of the customers came out of the bakery. Soon they were joined by customers from the other shops, a postman and various stray villagers, a housewife and two children, a local farmer, the man from the solicitor's office up the road. A few minutes ago, Angela would have said there was no one and nothing around except a few ducks. Now it was like an I-Spy of village life, with more and more people turning up to join the angry mob.

'That refugee woman. She took the cake.'

'Aw, leave her alone. It's for the kid. Can't you imagine what life's like for them?'

'She wanted money, she could go and do a day's work in the field. There's crops to pick. Half my potatoes rotted where they lay this year, no one wants to do it. They're too lazy.'

'I'm in Eye Tee,' said Angela.

They ignored her.

'Search her. See what else she's stolen.' This from a very well-presented woman emerging from behind the counter of a knickknack shop. Someone took Angela's bag.

'Leave her alone,' said the housewife. The woman's two children looked at Angela with such horrified sympathy that she couldn't bear it. She looked away.

Someone started searching through their bags. She hoped they wouldn't pat her down, horrible rough men feeling under her armpits and around her waist to see whether she had a half a dozen bath buns or a couple of pork chops tucked away.

Someone found something in one of the bags and held up the incriminating evidence, waving it triumphantly. Such a crowd had gathered, even Angela had to crane her neck to see. The mood turned hostile as soon as people saw it, and she wondered if something had been planted in the bag by the man whose fat hands had delved into its inner pockets and now aired its contents in front of the assembly.

'Quids,' said the man. 'Thousands and thousands of quids.'

There was a groany gasp from the villagers, as if this were a music hall act and the audience had just been given their cue to react.

'But we can't use them here,' said Angela. She was frightened.

'She's saving them? Stealing from us and she's *saving* her own money. What for? A house in France? A yacht on the Solent?'

'We thought they wouldn't accept it,' Angela said. It was so unfair.

'Course we will,' said the woman from the bakery, gently. 'Why wouldn't we?'

'Trade restrictions. You see, when we were in Slough—'

'Ah! Slough.'

'Look at her nail polish,' said the woman from the knickknack shop, bitterly. 'Might have known she'd been to *Slough*.'

'Stocking up on the latest fashions,' said the man from the solicitor's office. He obviously wasn't acquainted with the latest fashions, as Angela was wearing Maureen's khaki trousers and a long-sleeved stripy grey top with a teddy bear design embossed on it in pink.

'They won't let the likes of us in to Slough,' said one of the villagers.

'They don't approve of country people,' said another.

'No. They like the ones with money.'

'Perhaps she's a smuggler? All that money. Betraying her own kind.'

Just then, Maureen arrived, pushing her way through the crowd. 'What seems to be the trouble?' asked Maureen.

'Another one!' said a man.

'She stands accused of stealing a cream slice.'

'It was custard,' said Angela.

'I'm so sorry,' said Maureen. 'A misunderstanding. She's a bit... she's not very bright.'

Angela blushed. It was an awful betrayal. She'd managed to keep her chin up until then, but Maureen's words made her dissolve. And standing just in front of Angela, her back against Angela's thighs, her face towards the crowd as if she would fight any one of them, Christina now began to cry, too.

'I'm sorry,' Maureen said again. 'They're both a bit simple. I should never have left them.'

The crowd looked at Angela and Christina, both now grizzling, the custard slice still in Angela's hand, a preposterous trophy for which to risk prison or deportation. Most seemed satisfied with Maureen's explanation.

'Perhaps we can settle this?' said Maureen. 'Should we be paying a fine?'

Someone took the handfuls of currency they'd found in Angela's bag and divided it arbitrarily, about half of it for the village, the other half for Maureen. The woman from the bakery shook her head. 'I don't want it, duck. Leave them. Let them go on their way.' She went back inside to her pink pigs, her white mice, her cakes, her cobs and her bloomers.

There was a rumble of dissatisfaction from some sections of the crowd. This had been an entertaining spectacle; they didn't want it to end. They began to disagree about what should happen next.

'You should search 'em both,' one man suggested. 'And the kid.'

'Don't let 'em keep any of the money. It's got to have been stolen.'

'Gw'an, get out of here,' someone else said. 'Gw'an, thieves!'

'No, keep hold of them. Turn'm in to immigration.'

Something fell from Angela's bag and pinged on the ground as they tussled over it. It was the compass. The man from the solicitor's office bent and picked it up with exaggerated caution, as if he'd never seen a compass before and suspected necromancy.

It was at that point that an unlikely rescuer rode to their aid. A very large woman driving a horse and cart – and this was in a smart village in Somerset, where everyone who wanted a car had access to one – came thundering along at top speed, like the Scarlet Pimpernel arriving to rescue the aristocracy from the gallows.

'Save yourselves,' she yelled at Maureen, Angela and Christina, and stopped long enough to haul them in to the cart. As they thundered off again, she shouted, 'Cock-suckers,' at the villagers, who were obviously used to it because although they muttered a bit, they soon dispersed.

33 You Can Call Me Anna

Lucas was surprised when he opened his eyes and saw who was in his cell. He'd been surprised so often by visitors over the last few days that he shouldn't have been surprised any more. But he was.

'Mum?' he said. 'Mummy?' It had been so long since he'd said the word – not since he was a kid – that it seemed childish and out of time. Like asking for his blanky or his bockle or his potty.

'Hello, beautiful,' she said. She looked like she was made out of marzipan and Bailey's Irish Cream.

'Dad said you ran away.'

'Did he?'

'It's not true, then?'

'He actually used the word "ran"? He couldn't have said "walked"?'

She seemed amused. She smelled of the outside, like fresh rain on grass in summertime.

Lucas said, 'You look like Christmas but you smell like summer.'

She laughed. She said, 'This place is pretty dire, isn't it? Are you doing OK?'

'I'm alright.'

'Whose clothes are you wearing for goodness' sake?'

'I lost some weight since I came in here.'

'You got a fever?'

'I don't know. Maybe. Maybe don't come too close.'

'I thought we could do something with this place. Would you like that?'

'Blast the doors open, you mean?'

'I could paint you a doorway, here. You want to help me? You always liked painting when you were a kid.'

'I'm a bit dizzy now. You mind if I lie here for a bit?'

'I don't mind at all.'

'You prefer Mum or Mummy?'

'You can call me Anna.' She saw it wasn't the answer he wanted. 'Mummy, then.'

'You mind if I call you Mum?'

'Silly thing. You do what you want.' She looked around, as if she wanted to make sure they were alone. She said, 'It's your birthday in a couple of weeks.'

'Is it? I've lost track of time.'

'Let's see if we can finish this before then, hey?'

And so she started to paint on the wall. First she drew in the doorway, meticulously shading in the woodwork and the paintwork, so it looked 3D.

Lucas lay back. He felt very weak. It was a rotten situation but he was glad to have his mother here. She was a capable, reassuring woman, still beautiful. He was happy, for her sake, to see that she didn't seem to have aged a day since she ran, walked or was stolen away, twenty years ago.

'Mum?'

'Yes?'

But he didn't have a question for her. He'd just wanted to say the word. He put his head back on the blanket he was lying on, closed his eyes and drifted off to sleep.

34 Panther

Their rescuer shouted over the sound of the horse's hooves to say her name was Ruth and the horse was called Celeste. Maureen sat at the front on an uncomfortably narrow seat covered in hessian, her knees squeezed tightly together because there was not much room; Ruth had her thighs splayed open very wide, like an anxious would-be father trying to cool his testicles.

Angela and Christina shuddered and juddered in the cart behind them, giggling like innocent heroines in a Thomas Hardy novel just before the bad things start to happen to them.

'You might want to eat that cream slice or throw it away,' said Maureen, turning round.

'It's custard,' Angela said.

She handed it to Christina, who ate it, then licked her hand, then licked Angela's hand. Maureen handed out the wet wipes. Angela smiled and shrugged her shoulders at Christina while they cleaned up.

Ruth brought them to her home, which was a commune. It was a place, she explained, where women could live together in harmony, ecologically, with respect for their surroundings (although the 'cock-sucker' villagers were presumably exempt from that respect) and a love for nature. The life, said Ruth, was tough but rewarding. She hoped Angela and Maureen would consider joining them.

'It would be nice to rest for a while,' said Maureen. 'After that, we've got to press on.'

'We're just passing through,' said Angela.

Ruth showed them round what was essentially an encampment of about two dozen sturdy-looking olive green army tents pitched in a ring, and a few tumbledown stone buildings. The place smelled of bonfires, as did the women living there. Their unfortunate existence seemed to involve sitting on the floor and stirring big iron pots of bean stew over an open fire.

Maureen looked in her handbag. 'Thanks so much for helping us out,' she said to Ruth. 'I wish we had something to give you. A little token.' She sifted through the treasures she kept in there – wet wipes, antiseptic hand wash, some satsumas, several packets of raisins. Angela remembered the loaf of bread in her bag and brought that out. But Ruth looked disdainful and glanced over to where women were baking gritty flat bread on hot stones.

'Actually, there is something,' said Ruth. 'That money you had. We could do with some of it, to build a school here.'

Angela felt her heart beat faster, her system flooding with adrenaline. Maureen smiled a warm and appreciative smile. She held Ruth's gaze for a few moments. She said nothing. They went and sat by one of the bonfires and had a cup of smoky tea. Maureen handed round the raisins. Angela saw a few of the women looking with longing at the bread in her bag but she wasn't sure that Ruth would approve if she shared it out and she didn't want to push it.

'Well,' said Maureen after a while. 'Thanks for the tea. I suppose we'd better be heading off.'

'Where you heading?'

'Westerly.'

'To Cornwall?'

'We've got family there. Angela's mother-in-law. My father.'

'You're not heading for Wales, are you? You'll never make it.'

'Are they dangerous, the Welsh?' Angela asked.

'Oh no. They're lovely people. But you'll never get across. They took the bridge down after partition.'

'We're heading for Cornwall,' Maureen assured her. 'Which way would you suggest?'

Ruth stood, put her hand on Maureen's shoulder and pointed the way. 'You take that road, it snakes a bit. Follow it as far as you can, 'til you reach the crossroads. Go straight over, keep on going. Be careful of the UN forces, the peacekeepers. You can't trust them. Look out for the white vehicles, the meat-fed foreign men spending money on trashy women in the bars, and avoid them. Other than that, you can't go wrong, really – you can navigate by the sun.'

'Thanks,' said Maureen, 'Angela's got a compass.'

'Actually?' said Angela, getting to her feet. Everyone ignored her.

'Course,' said Ruth. 'You can't go *now*.'

She looked stern. The women of the camp were standing around, blocking the way out of the camp. Perhaps it was unintentional. But there was a sense that it was not going to be easy to leave this place.

'They're expecting us,' said Angela. 'They'll be worried.'

'It's nearly nightfall. The animals are on the prowl.'

The sheep? The donkeys? The cows? Angela failed to disguise a giggle.

'It's a full moon tonight,' Ruth said. 'Didn't you notice?'

'Won't that help us?' Angela asked. 'There aren't that many clouds. We should be able to see the way.'

'No. You don't understand. There are wild animals around here, lions and tigers and that. They can smell us. Most of the women are menstruating.'

'Oh, I see,' said Maureen. Her face seemed to harden and thicken, like a speeded up demonstration of the effects of sun damage. Perhaps it was the exposure to the country air. Perhaps it was Ruth's explanation about why they shouldn't leave. Maureen seemed to age about five years.

'I thought it was a myth,' said Angela. 'About the animals?'

'After that fella up London let 'em all out from Regent's Park Zoo, everyone had to have a turn, didn't they? Most of the ones round here are from Bristol Zoo, though they say the elephants might be from Paignton.'

'But I thought they'd perished. Or that even if they survived, they hid away from human contact.'

'C'mere, Panther,' Ruth called to an unfeline-looking woman standing across the way.

Panther ambled over. She knew what Ruth was going to tell her to do. She didn't wait to be asked, she hitched up her dress. She wasn't wearing knickers, (perhaps underwear was unecological?) but the fact barely registered with Angela because of what she saw. The poor woman had been hideously scarred, with slashes and claw marks on her belly and chunks of her flesh missing. She had been attacked by a ferocious creature. A big cat, perhaps – maybe even a… Angela looked at the evidence and understood the significance of the woman's name, although not the wisdom of it. She herself might otherwise have ended up being called Chicken Pox.

It was settled that Maureen, Angela and Christina would stay in the camp that night, for their own safety and to help with guard duty. The bonfires had practical applications that extended beyond cooking. Potential predators were frightened of fire, so Ruth said.

'How awful, poor Panther,' Angela said to Ruth. 'She'll never recover from those scars.'

'That's how we felt, at first. Now we embrace it. Come along to the ceremony tonight. You'll see what I mean.'

They were assigned a tent to stay in and given a bowl of warm water so they could wash before dinner.

'I think we're in trouble,' said Maureen.

'It's not the worst we've faced.'

'I don't want to be melodramatic about it. But this place gives me the creeps.'

'It's your mind playing tricks. You're worrying because we're getting closer to Cornwall and there's so many things can still go wrong.'

'Angela, I love you very much. You're like family to me. You'll take care of Christina, won't you, if anything does happen. Having her has been the greatest, the best thing in my life. And it's nothing unusual, to have a child. Something doesn't have to be unusual to be special, remember that. Anyone who gets up in time can watch the sun rise and that can be the most magnificent and moving sight in the world, and yet it's freely available to anyone.'

'Except blind people. And people in underground prisons.'

'Yes, OK.'

They linked arms with Christina between them, and they stepped out of the tent like a six-legged creature; separation unthinkable, if not impossible.

'Do you eat pigs?' Ruth asked them when they got to the food tent.

Most people in London were not flesh eaters. They were upset by it. As a general rule, they didn't eat pigs, people, cats, dogs, peacocks, rats, squirrels, chickens. They had fish from their city's waterways and fresh vegetables grown in the acres of park lands across the city. They consumed nothing with legs.

Maureen and Angela drank a lot of wine with their meal, unused to the farmyard stench of the cooked flesh, the women tearing at it like animals. This place was full of stinks. There was the droopy flesh of the women, smelling as if they had just got out of bed and hadn't had a shower yet; not disgusting but rather too intimate. The women didn't believe in chemicals for deodorant. They didn't even use protective sun tan lotion, so their skin was striped; suntanned then pale, suntanned then pale, according to the positioning of their clothing during previous exposure to the sun.

'You're outsiders, like us,' Ruth said after the meal. 'I think you'll like the ceremony. This way please.'

She walked them through the camp towards one of the tilted, inhospitable-looking stone buildings. With the smoke, the tilting, the dazed feeling caused by the consumption of the wine, the awful oinking conversations of pigs in nearby pens who must have been able to smell the roast flesh of their late companion, it was like walking around in the immediate aftermath of something terrible – more terrible than dinner had been, even.

'Whatever they're going to do, I think we have to try and protect Christina from seeing it,' said Maureen.

'It's so smoky, she won't be able to help closing her eyes,' Angela said.

They were led inside what must have been the smokiest place in the camp. Ruth motioned for them to follow the example of other women who queued up to dip a bowl into a stone tank filled with water, then removed or pulled aside or pulled up or down whatever they were wearing on their top halves, and splashed the water over themselves to wash their hands, arms and upper torsos, then readjusted their clothing and went into the next room.

Angela had been trying not to stare, to preserve the other women's modesty, but Maureen nudged her. Angela looked. She saw that some of the women's bodies had been scarified. Flowers, fish, trees, butterflies had been carved into the skin on their arms and backs.

It should have prepared her for what was to come but she had to struggle to keep from vomiting. In the centre of the room she saw a woman, with all the artistry of a ten-year-old trying her hand at lino cutting, begin to mark the flesh of a younger woman, about eighteen years old.

'Stay still now, Connie. You're doing a grand job,' the woman soothed as she worked on her client's flesh. 'That's it. That's a girl.'

Connie lay on a cloth on some hay bales, face down, arms bare. Angela could not recall witnessing a scene before that cried out so blatantly for the distribution of Maureen's wet wipes. Though the alcohol in the little tissues would probably smart if they came in contact with the skin so perhaps the filthy-looking sponge employed to wipe away the blood would do just as well in the circumstances – these people were the experts, after all.

What the cutter lacked in artistic execution she more than made up for in speed and deftness, slicing through the skin, stripping out gobbets of flesh, halting the process occasionally to press on the bleeding wound with the sponge, then slicing again, stripping away the unwanted bits of the young woman and throwing them into a dish.

'We throw the contents of the dish to the wild animals,' Ruth confided. She was whispering, as if feeding human flesh to lions and tigers and pumas was such a good idea that she didn't want everyone to hear in case they should try to copy it.

'Surely it attracts them?'

'You have to embrace the thing you fear. Run towards it. We spend our whole time in this crazy consumerist society trying to protect ourselves from what frightens us. We build walls around us. We put up barriers between ourselves and nature. We put layers of meaning between each other; social constructs, manners, class systems, gender definitions.'

'Oh, I see.'

'Since we've been doing this, we haven't had a single attack.'

Angela thought that any puma coming within a whisker of this place would be so freaked out by the crazy women and their offerings of their own flesh served up in an earthenware dish that it would probably turn and run as fast as it could to the nearest village and open a cake shop and never even complain if anyone came in and helped themselves to a custard slice without paying.

'It subdues them?' she asked Ruth. 'Shows them who's boss?'

'No. They go and attack the villagers. They don't bother with us.'

Angela didn't get the chance to ask any more questions because just then, the men came. There was a lot of shouting and confusion – drunken men's voices complaining loudly about the ecological toilet arrangements and the chanting at the camp. They seemed not to know about the flesh-feeding arrangements.

'Your chantin' stirs up the beasts.'

'Never heard of flushing toilets?'

'Dirty shitting stinkers!'

'Stinkers! Stinking bitching stinkers.'

'It's your chantin' makes them attack.'

'Hags.'

'C'm out, c'm out, c'm out!'

'C'm out!'

The women were fierce and brave. They armed themselves with stones and went out to meet the men with flaming torches made from alcohol-soaked rags on sticks which they ignited by dipping them into the bonfires. But the men had guns, tasers, mobile phones, electric torches, cars, motorbikes, even (though it was not clear why they should be needed on this occasion) MP3 players. It was an unequal contest.

Angela couldn't see Maureen anywhere. She took Christina's hand and ran. She hid with her in the hollowed out base of a tree which had hand-carved chairs arranged in a rough semi-circle in front of it. Presumably it had been conceived as a picnic area, though it might have been anything from an al fresco courtroom to a birthing room to a hairdressing salon. No, not a salon.

Angela tried to transmit thoughts to Maureen to guide her to where they were hiding. Maybe it worked because now Maureen was running towards them. 'Christina!' she shouted. 'Angela!'

Just then, one of the men stepped out with his gun drawn and shouted, 'Stop!'

Maureen, Ruth and some of the others turned to face the men. They lined up and walked backwards, slowly, until they were as far back as they could go, with the hand-carved chairs behind them. They were about two feet in front of where Angela and Christina were hiding.

'You've got illegals here. Give 'em over, we're turning 'em in.'

'No,' said Ruth. 'You'll have to kill us first.' A few of the men sniggered a bit at that but she continued, magnificent in her defiance: 'I will never betray a woman who has sought sanctuary from us.'

'I'm sure we can sort this out, like reasonable adults,' Maureen said, very calm. Even if the men didn't recognise Maureen from the incident outside the bakery, her non-commune garb advertised her status as an outsider. She was the only woman in view of the men who was not wearing a dress fashioned out of home-woven sacking. Her hair was shiny and furthermore – and Angela could not tell which way the wind was blowing but the men were standing pretty close – she would be the only one would not smell as if she had been smoked like a kipper; she would be smelling of hand cream and mints.

'She's got money,' said Ruth. 'Why don't you take that?'

Angela wondered what Ruth had been before she'd dropped out of society. Probably not a trained negotiator.

Maureen was close enough to be able to hear if Angela called out to her. Angela knew she shouldn't do it because then she and Christina would also be discovered. But wouldn't it be the right thing to do, to climb out of the tree and stand shoulder to shoulder with her friend? She probably would have done – she'd rather have stuck with Maureen than risk being left alone – if it hadn't been for Christina. She had to protect Christina.

She could see Maureen shifting about, her weight on her left foot, her right foot kicking back and forward, circling round in the dirt. If it was a nervous tic that betrayed her terror, outwardly, she was calm.

'Where's the money, then?' asked the leader of the mob from the village.

Maureen nodded her head towards the tent where they had left their luggage. Two men accompanied her to the tent. The leader and the other men remained with Ruth and the other women, guns drawn.

'You think she can give them the slip?' she heard Panther whisper to Ruth.

'Why should they care if we've got refugees here or not? It's no business of theirs. They'll get their hands on the money, they'll feel so bloody pleased with themselves, they'll leave us – and her – alone.'

Silence for a few minutes, then three gunshots, then the incongruous sound of a mobile phone ringing in the ruined night. Angela heard the leader of the mob answer the phone, then he turned to the others and said, 'Let's go.'

They went, just like that.

'Go and see if Maureen's alright,' Ruth said to Panther.

Angela remained hidden with Christina. The metallic smell of fired shotgun cartridges hung in the air. The whole camp had stunk of blood, pig shit, ecological toilet shit, piss and bonfires, even before the men had arrived. It was not possible for Angela to discern from the olefactory clues available whether anyone had been injured or killed. She desperately, desperately hoped not.

After about five minutes more, Panther returned and reported to Ruth. 'No sign of her.'

A pause, then Ruth asked, so casually that Angela knew she was ashamed of herself for saying it: 'And the money?'

'No. Her handbag was there, but it was empty and tipped upside down. A packet of wet wipes and three satsumas, that's all that was left behind.'

'What about the girls?'

'I haven't seen them since the trouble started. They must of run.'

'Or been taken.'

'That's it, then. Poor things. They won't get far.'

'They were a bit simple. Maureen said as much when I picked them up in the village. I wish I'd never brought them here.'

'It's not your fault, Ruth.'

'I'll go out tomorrow in the cart, have a look for them. Maureen, too.'

'I don't think you'll find Maureen,' Panther said.

They stood for a few moments, then Panther gave Ruth a hug and walked away. Ruth stood and looked at the moon for a few minutes. Then she walked away, in a different direction.

Angela waited until just before dawn. Christina had fallen asleep. She stroked Christine's face and rubbed her hands to wake her, then they crawled out of the hiding place together. The moon and the stars were shining on the patch of dirt where Maureen had stood before she was taken away. Angela saw that Maureen had left something for them, a message so they'd know she'd known they were hiding two feet from her, and that she loved them. It was a heart shape, traced on the ground with her foot, over and over, as the men had pointed their guns at her.

Angela crept back to the tent to retrieve her bag. Every time she stepped on something that crunched or gave way under her feet – distressingly often – she wondered whether she might be stepping on the remains of other women Ruth had 'helped'. When she got to the tent, she found that Maureen had left them more than just a packet of wet wipes and three satsumas. Panther had either failed to notice or not bothered to mention

223

that she had also left behind a tube of toffees, some squares of toilet paper, five pens, an emery board, a tube of Nivea hand cream, half a packet of mints and the letter from Jesmond with the *Gauzy Love Song* poem written on it in blue ink. Angela took this legacy, her bag of Maureen's clothes, Christina's Bratz doll, and Christina, and slipped out of the camp.

As they passed an untended bonfire, Christina reached out and dropped the Bratz doll into it. A veil of thick smoke reached up into the sky behind them. It might have symbolised Maureen's departed soul climbing to heaven, if Angela believed in such things.

35 Little Things

'The thing is,' the interviewer said. 'I feel you're wasting my time.'

It was the young one, Terry Gator. In spite of what had happened between them, Lucas still quite liked him – or at any rate, he preferred him to the older man – but this statement was unfair in every way. Just for starters, it was the interviewer who was so obviously wasting Lucas's time. If he wasn't required to be in here, kept prisoner by locked doors and barred windows, Lucas would be using his allocated hours quite differently. He would be at home with Angela.

He wished he had cherished every moment as it had occurred, not wasted his life in regrets. He hadn't realised that the ordinary little things that happened, the ones that took place between the big events while waiting for something more exciting to happen – they were the most important, after all. If he'd had a pen, he might have written that down, not realising that others had discovered it before him and that others would discover it after him.

He had no pen. He had no one to tell what he had learned while enduring the worst kinds of unpleasantness that could be inflicted by one person on another. Instead, he thought about Angela, and where she might be now in her journey towards freedom.

36 Sticky Toffee Pudding

Angela was very, very hungry. When she was a child, her preoccupations had included worrying about whether an apple pip really could grow into a tree in a person's stomach, wondering whatever happened to the *Marie Celeste*, wondering how the Egyptians had built the pyramids, things like that – big problems, general problems, other people's problems. Now she was older, she was more selfish. She just worried about herself and Christina.

She assumed Christina was as hungry as she was. But the child didn't moan about it, either because she was wondering how the Egyptians built the pyramids or because she didn't have the means to complain. It was probably the latter. Still, she always acquiesced so sweetly in every situation. She didn't drum her heels or kick her legs. She didn't squawk wordlessly, like a pterosaur or some other prehistoric angry thing. She just endured. Angela wouldn't have wished this on any kid but if she had to have a kid with her on a journey through hell, she wouldn't find a better companion than Christina.

Angela thought about how badly Lucas used to behave when his blood sugar plummeted. If dinner was even so much as an hour late, he'd get cross, without knowing why, until she gave him a cracker or some crisps or some other snack to keep him going. She tried not to think about Lucas, it would set her off again. She hoped that wherever he was, he knew that she was thinking about him. It hadn't been a particularly nice thought but that didn't matter. They loved each other. They didn't need to be nice to each other all the time. They'd signed up for the long haul.

They must not be far from the moor. They had walked for days. Their feet were swollen and hurting and they were hungry. It had started raining. She saw a tavern – a pub, really, although it presented itself as terribly olde worlde – and brought Christina inside to sit by the fire and warm up. If the landlord spotted that they hadn't bought a drink or anything to eat and he came over and threw them out, well, OK. They would get up again and move on.

'Hey there,' said a man, a customer, about Lucas's age. Healthy-looking. 'Can I get you girls a drink?'

'Oh no. It's OK.'

'Go on. A coke or something. For the little one.'

They settled on orange juice for both of them. He brought two glasses of it, and a beer for himself, and then a girl of about fourteen who was waitressing brought along two big plates of egg and chips and a sticky toffee pudding for Christina. Their benefactor shrugged and

228

smiled. He was so nice about it, it was clear that he could see how desperately hungry they were.

Christina fell on the food as soon as it was set down in front of her. Angela wasn't far behind.

'Where you from?' he asked.

'London.'

'Cockneys? I should have got you jellied eels.'

'Do they sell them here?'

'No.' He laughed.

She cheered up a bit and laughed along with him. 'You live round here?'

'Not far. I live up at the base.'

'You're a soldier.'

'Do I look French? No, I'm a mechanic. I work on the vehicles there.'

'I heard they were bad people.'

'There's a bit of good in everyone. Wouldn't you say?'

They sat in silence while Angela and Christina finished their meal. Then he said, 'So where you gonna sleep tonight?'

Angela thought, oh, here it comes. Still, he's quite nice looking and he's been kind to us. I could sleep with him and maybe he'd give us some money and some food for the journey. It wouldn't be so bad, so long as Christina didn't have to watch it.

He said, 'I know a place, a little bed and breakfast. It's about twenty miles from here, on the moor. It's a nice place. I know the owner. You fancy it?'

She thought it might be nice to have sex with someone. She should look at it like that, instead of being

229

the victim. She should try and make the most of it. It was what liberated women did, by choice. A warm bath, a warm bed, sex with a man. At least she had something to sell, she should be grateful for that. Then in the morning, they'd have breakfast. Orange juice and eggs and a couple of rounds of toast. She thought, if he gives us a lift as far as the border, tomorrow I'll be in Cornwall and we can start our new life.

'OK,' she said.

'Come on, then,' he said. He looked really pleased. Maybe prostitutes had turned him down in the past. 'It won't be busy. They hardly get any customers cause of the wild animals. She's a really nice lady, runs it. She'll love the little girl.'

He got up and jingled his car keys and went to settle the bill. The young waitress stood at the bar and stared at them as if she guessed the nature of the transaction that had just taken place, and thought less of Angela for it. Put yourself in my shoes, thought Angela, then you can go ahead and judge me, you little bitch. But then the girl came over with two packets of pork scratchings and a My Little Pony key ring, which she took from her purse and offered to Christina with a shy smile. 'Good luck,' she said. And Angela said, 'Thank you,' and felt really bad.

He took them out to the truck he was driving and helped them into the cab. He said his name was Dave. Angela thought, well, this is kind of funny. It's the first date I've ever been on with a man.

There was no traffic on the roads except for the camouflaged armoured vehicles of the security forces and one white jeep belonging to one of the dozens of NGOs operating in the area. It came up behind them very fast, headlights flashing, the sneering sound of a horn with a hand pressed hard on it growing louder and louder as the driver approached.

'Alright, alright,' said Dave, pulling over. Angela hunched down in her seat and put her arms around Christina, thinking they were going to be stopped and questioned. But the jeep overtook and kept on going. 'In a hurry for a big night out,' Dave said, pulling out and driving off again, sedately. The brake lights of the jeep whizzed ahead of them and then disappeared, two red rockets in the damp night.

About halfway through the journey, Christina was sick down herself – it was all yellow. Dave smiled sympathetically and handed Angela an oily-looking hand towel so she could wipe Christina down. He kept driving and sang a song about chickens while she changed Christina's top and trousers for cleaner ones from the rucksack. She did the harmonies on the chicken song and he said she had a really nice voice. He handed her a bottle of water so she could hold Christina's shoes out the window and wash them off.

She thought, I expect this is what it's like being a family. She was so, so sorry she had never had a baby with Lucas. This was lovely, even though technically-speaking she was prostituting herself for two plates of egg and chips, two glasses of orange juice, a sticky toffee pudding and whatever cash Dave had on him for the next stage of the journey.

After they had been driving for about half an hour, they reached a barrier across a narrow lane leading across the moor, and Dave stopped.

'Well,' he said. 'Here we are. I'm sorry, I can't drive you any further. I'm not supposed to take the truck in there. Well, I can't anyway, with the barrier. It's about quarter of a mile up there on the right – Honeysuckle Cottage. I'll walk you up there. Then Mandy'll look after you. When she knows I've sent you, she'll put out the flags.'

'Who?'

'Mandy. The owner of the B&B. I fixed her engine once, when she was broken down along here, at the side of the road. She'll give you a bed for the night. Then after that, you're on your own and I don't envy you. But it's not far to the border and they don't guard this side. You might be alright. Come on, then. You want to take the littl'un and I'll carry the bag?'

So she was not being called upon to sleep with him for money? The shock of it made her ungracious. She said, 'You don't need to come any further. I'll be OK.'

'If I give you my card, will you ring me when you get to Cornwall, so I know you've made it?'

She had been wrong about him. She should have been much more grateful, all the way along, but she had thought she was going to have to settle their debt in the old fashioned way. She hadn't known he was just being kind. Had she been rude to him? He must think she was half-witted. Had she let on that she'd thought she'd have to sleep with him? She was so confused that she was quite adamant that he must not accompany them to the bed and breakfast. He had done enough. He had driven all this way and now he had to drive back again. It was late. Maybe he had a wife or someone at home, waiting. She would walk the last little bit alone, thank you very much.

He wasn't very happy about that but she was as prim and firm about it as she might have been in other circumstances if he had actually propositioned her.

'Well, I s'pose you've managed this far without me.' He put some money into her hand, as she knew he would. 'I know you won't like taking it,' he said. 'But you can pay it back when you're on your feet again. Or even better, give it to someone else who needs it.'

He didn't say that his sister had once found herself in the same position or that his wife was a refugee or his parents had come from Afghanistan fifty years before or anything like that. It seemed he didn't need a special reason. He just wanted to be kind.

'Goodbye, littl'un,' he said to Christina, bending down so the child could see his face properly.

'See that?' said Angela. 'She smiled. She doesn't do that for everyone. It means she likes you.'

He took her hand, not quite a handshake, more of a clasp, holding her left hand with his right hand for a brief moment, to say goodbye.

'Actually,' Angela said. 'It's my birthday today.'

'Is it?' He looked really sad when she said that. 'How old are you, then?'

'Twenty-one.'

233

'Happy birthday.'

'Thanks.'

He watched them walk a little way up the unlit road to their destination. When they turned the corner out of sight, they heard him toot the horn and drive away. They kept walking. Angela felt quite cheerful. She thought that everything was going to turn out right.

37 Dreams

'A few people have been to visit me here,' said Lucas to his mother. 'Why didn't my father come?'

'He did,' said Anna. 'You've been in a pretty bad way: feverish, hallucinating. Perhaps you didn't know him when he was here.'

'Angela's the one person I don't want to see. I hope she's safe somewhere. I don't want her to show up here.'

'I know.'

'You think we should never have talked about going to Cornwall?'

'Dreams create possibilities,' Anna said. 'When you dream, you launch something that goes out into the world, and if you don't go with it, it'll go without you.'

'So if you don't dream, everything stays the same?'

'You can't ever have that. It isn't just your dreams, there's other people's.'

'I did something silly. There was this woman, Joanna Jones…'

'We've all done something silly at some point, Lucas. Don't worry about it. You like the picture?'

He was worried about Angela. Where was she now?

38 Honeysuckle Cottage

Honeysuckle Cottage was a lovely-looking place. There was a little gate that clinked as Angela opened it, and a path that led up to the cottage through a slightly overgrown garden. There was something that registered as not quite right about it as she walked towards it but she was so tired and achey, all she could think about was getting inside and introducing herself to Mandy, and having a bath and falling in to bed and sleeping all night.

She rang the doorbell. No answer. Then she realised what was wrong about it. There were no lights on in the cottage. The place didn't look derelict but it did look deserted. She walked up to a window and stared in at the empty interior. She tried the gate that led to the back garden and might have given her access to the back door but it was locked.

She went to the front door again, she rang the doorbell and knocked the dolphin-shaped brass knocker and she banged with her fists on the door. If Mandy had only popped to the shops, she would wait. But there was dust on the front door. Leaves had blown in piles against the doorstep. It looked as if, wherever Mandy had popped to, she would not be coming back until the bed and breakfast season started again and custom picked up a bit – which might take years, not months. At any rate, however long it took, it would be too long to wait.

She went round and tried all the windows at the front, in case one of them was not secured properly and she could get in – or squeeze Christina in, and get her to come round and open the front door – and they could make themselves at home. She didn't want to break a window; that was no way to repay a friend of Dave's, after he had been so helpful. Mandy would have helped them, if she'd been here. Angela was sure of it because Dave had been so sure. She wished she had asked him more about himself – asked him anything, in fact – so that she could reflect on it on the long journey ahead and take comfort in the things that he was sure of and be sure about them herself.

It was cold. There seemed little point in lying down to sleep in the front garden of the cottage. It was probably better to keep walking. It would keep them warm and take them nearer to their destination.

They walked, hand in hand. Sometimes she lifted Christina on to her back and carried her, sometimes she had to put her down and get her to walk by herself. The child was almost delirious with tiredness. It amounted to mistreatment. She couldn't think why they had ever thought it would be a good idea to bring the child along. And yet, without Christina, she would not have been nearly so well-treated herself, and she would not now be motivated to keep going on this terrible journey. So, although it sounded slightly dramatic to say it, she felt that Christina had saved her life.

Being on the moor was like wandering in a lost land where dinosaurs roamed. It was like going back to the beginning of time. Her legs were chafing, she had blisters on her feet, she was thirsty. She was staying alive for the child, otherwise she'd have been tempted to lie down and stay lying down. She walked slowly, singing, counting aloud, the child bumping on her back. They had very little sleep. It was important to keep marching on. Sometimes she saw a landmark and she was sure she had seen it before. Sometimes she was part of the scenery; she was a tree, walking. Still she kept going forward.

Sometimes she talked aloud. Sometimes she carried on a conversation with Lucas in her head. If there were dangerous animals at large, she never saw one. She saw red deer, sheep, a few ponies. Once, while she knelt to collect water from a stream, she had a glimpse of a giraffe in the distance, nibbling at leaves in the tree tops, that was all. Poor thing, you're a long way from home, she thought. Whether she was communicating with the giraffe or it was communicating with her, she couldn't tell.

She thought about Jesmond and the woman he had loved. She thought about her parents and Maureen. She thought about Lucas, of course. Sometimes she talked to them, sometimes she turned ideas about them over in her head, almost like a meditation. It made no difference – even to Christina, apparently – whether she spoke aloud or not, and it began to make no difference to her. She kept expecting to see Maureen. It seemed entirely possible that Maureen had not been shot or taken by immigration and deported but was wandering on the moor, not too far away. Angela imagined running into her: 'What a lovely surprise!' She would give Maureen the one remaining satsuma (or had Christina eaten it, she couldn't remember, she was too tired to check), they would put their arms around each other, they would put their heads together to make a plan. They would draw strength from each other.

The effect of walking on the moor, lost and half out of her mind with tiredness, was like putting a kaleidoscope to her memories. Several people fractured into dozens, then the mechanism changed again and all the people she had ever met and cared about merged into one companion walking beside her, urging her and Christina on. The little child was such a light weight to carry, and so quiet, Angela wondered sometimes if she might be dead.

She walked through a field of purple lupins. She couldn't tell whether she was seeing the lupins or imagining them, or remembering them. She liked blue flowers: delphiniums, cornflowers, hyacinths, hydrangeas, bluebells, irises, violets, lupins. The sort of blue flowers whose colours are shown up most vividly next to yellow or gold. Then, as if she'd made it happen by thinking about it, she saw something, some patches of gold moving about among the blue flowers.

As she got closer, she saw that it was a wounded giraffe lying on the ground, one foreleg blasted off just under the knee. There was a smoky, gunpowder smell near where the giraffe lay and a sweet smell of blood, as if someone had let off a firework in a butcher's shop. There was no sign of hunters, so perhaps it had triggered a primitive trap, or stepped on unexploded ordinance from ranges used nearby for practice by the British army before partition. Angela got close to the poor, wounded creature, saw its ears, shaped like the velvet flower spikes on a lupin, saw its eyes, big and frightened, like a cow's. It shuddered and twitched. She felt she ought to put it out of its misery. But how? Take a rock and club it to death? She wasn't sure that Christina would understand if she saw her do that. Poison it? Smother it? She had no poison with her. She had no pillow, either. Should she pinch its nostrils together, clamp its jaw? She had no weapons, conventional or otherwise. Wasn't it customary to slay a dragon by piercing its eye with a sword? At fifteen feet tall, surely the giraffe was almost the same size as a dragon. Angela had camping cutlery with her somewhere in Maureen's rucksack, a knife and a spork, but couldn't imagine doing the giraffe to death with those implements, she and Christina working together to stab it through a big heart that was roughly the same size as a man's head and just as heavy. And how long would it take to dig a grave for a giraffe using only a spork? She couldn't say. Couldn't even estimate it.

The giraffe smelled like horses, it was mooing, it was covered in sweat. Angela was worried about getting too close in case it should kick at them with its hooves, thrash about or rear up and fall again and crush them. She didn't want to look at it suffering but she forced herself to do it. She put her arms around its long, dinosaur neck and lay down next to it, Christina beside her. Without the benefit of a formal education she had no idea whether anyone else had ever hypothesised that the long-necked plesiosaurs on display in museums might be giraffe skeletons that had been put back together wrongly, and assigned drab green skins and small, mean eyes instead of the beautiful reticulated gold patterned hide and the big, kind eyes they had been born with.

How long could she lie there holding the creature's neck? If only Christina's tears could heal the creature's wounds. She willed it to haul itself to its feet again and lope three-legged across the moor, like a fashionably upholstered milking stool. But it would no more do that than grow wings and fly them all to Cornwall, wisps of clouds clinging round its head like a silly bonnet. The giraffe had died.

Angela stood up, picked Christina up, kept walking. She didn't look back, whether because she was frightened of seeing crows pecking at the giraffe's wounds, or whether because she might have seen that there were no lupins, there was no giraffe, just the moor, bleak and boring and endless, stretching out behind her as it stretched out in front of her.

In her mind, she had given up. But her body kept on going. She knew it because she heard the swish as her feet walked through the long, damp grass, the pretty little wild yellow and purple flowers: yellow pimpernel, cowslip, lesser celandine, wild parsnip, archangel, birdsfoot trefoil, the mallow, the yarrow, the speedwell, sorrel and clover, the bracken, the heather, the grasses, the butterflies. She had never seen so many butterflies.

39   Through the Doorway

Anna Gray was putting the finishing touches to the project in Lucas's prison cell. She had painted the doorway, the lovely view through it into the countryside. Now she was drawing in the details, the pretty little yellow and purple wild flowers, the bracken, the heather, the butterflies. In the distance, she had painted a woman and a child. And a sign, 'Welcome to Cornwall'.

'Are you ready, Lucas?' Anna said. 'You know what day it is?'

'My birthday?'

'It's such a strange thing, giving birth. I'm sorry you'll never experience it. It's the end of something, the start of something. Hurts like hell, mind you.'

They had burst Lucas's left eardrum. It was bleeding. It hurt like hell.

Lucas looked through the doorway and saw the woman in the painting. 'Is it Angela?' When he spoke, the woman seemed to turn towards him. The child too.

He was frightened that they would run towards him. He shouted, 'No! Keep going. You're not safe until you get there.' He was very weak. 'Is it Angela?' he asked again.

'Why don't you step through the doorway,' Anna said. 'You can go and meet her, if you like.'

So he did.

Epilogue

The Disappeared by Jason Prince

Jason stood on the stage in the crowded underground venue. He blinked several times. It was an affectation, a way of suggesting that he had just woken up, that he existed only in the presence of his audience and the rest of the time, he slept. He had a handsome goatee beard, much admired but never imitated. He stroked the beard once or twice, as if his chin functioned like a soap dispenser in a public toilet, and that by plucking at it with his fingers, the words required to recite his poem would be deposited in the palm of his hand. He hooked his thumb into the pocket of his jeans and spoke softly without notes:

The Disappeared

Our fathers who artlessly
protested the erosion of their freedom;
sitting around, singing songs, writing
poems, and sometimes even visiting
the theatre. While behind the scenes,
grey government mice nibbled

at the rights in the constitution, disconnecting
the cables and burning the place down.
Like children making snowflakes to decorate
a classroom, the mice men took a million snips
at the paperwork, then held up the results to show
the holes. Proudly. There are no more classrooms.
The curtains came down on the theatre, and stayed
down. Songs suppressed, freedom curtailed,
poetry driven underground.

If you arrest everyone as a terrorist or a paedophile,
eventually there's no one left. And while the
considerable burden of keeping elderly people
in care homes has gone away, enriching
the welfare state, there's no one left to educate
the children. Where are the wise men?
Where are the women? Who is there to ensure
the welfare of the state?

Our fathers taken away. Our mothers fading away.
Some families fleeing to the promised lands, to
Cornwall, Liverpool, Scotland, Australia and the rest.
No one returns. Not so much as a postcard
to help us gauge whether the escape has been
a success. We just have to guess.
After partition, parting. What can we do to protest?
The protester's life is invariably cut short by a misplaced
full stop. I wish. I wish I could.
But what?

By the same author

ALISON WONDERLAND
Only occasionally does a piece of fiction leap out and demand immediate cult status. Alison Wonderland is one.
The Times

Smith is gin-and-tonic funny.
Booklist

BEING LIGHT
Smith has a keen eye for material details, but her prose is lucid and uncluttered by heavy description. Imagine a satire on Cool Britannia made by the Coen Brothers.
Times Literary Supplement

This is a novel in which the ordinary and the unusual are constantly juxtaposed in various idiosyncratic characters... Its airy quirkiness is a delight.
The Times

A screwball comedy that really works.
The Independent

THE EMILY CASTLES MYSTERY SERIES
Helen Smith is a master story-teller.
Socrates Book Reviews

About the author

 Helen Smith is a novelist and playwright and the recipient of an Arts Council of England Award. In addition to *Being Light*, she is the author of *Alison Wonderland*, *The Miracle Inspector*, The Emily Castles mystery series and two children's books..

Made in the USA
Lexington, KY
18 March 2017